Tales From Colonia Popular

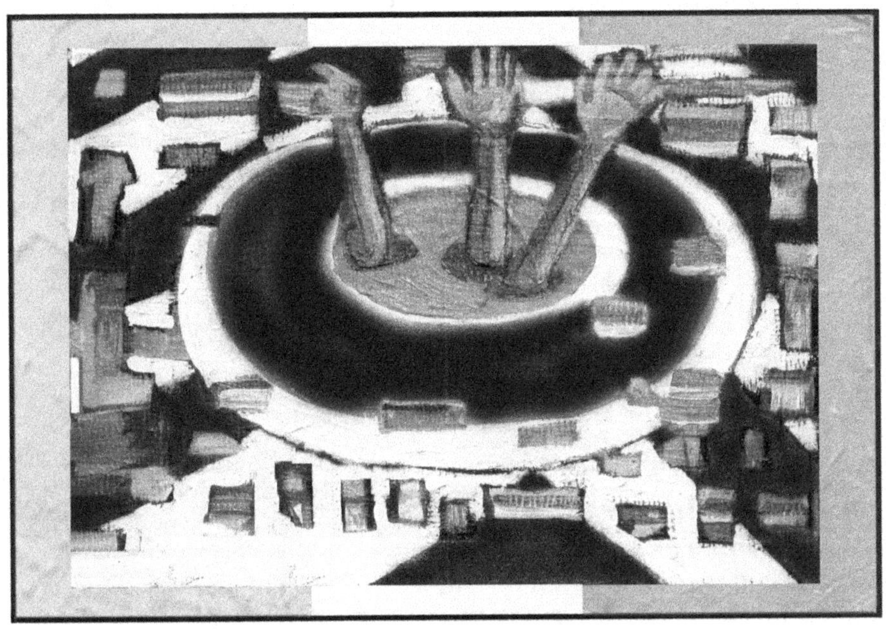

Tamar Diana Wilson

Plain View Press
P. O. 42255
Austin, TX 78704

plainviewpress.net
sb@plainviewpress.net
1-512-441-2452

ISBN: 978-1-891386-19-0
Library of Congress Number: 2009921665

Cover art "The Struggle" by Natasha Mayers
Cover design by Susan Bright

Acknowledgments

I would like to acknowledge the following publications in which these stories first appeared:
"Only Chiapas" was first published in *Struggle*, 1995 (Summer-Fall);
"La Rodina" was first published in *Anthropology and Humanism Quarterly*. 1992. 17(3/4): 66-71.

I would like to thank Tim Hall, editor of *Struggle* for his constant encouragement to publish my work. I would also like to thank the publishers of *Anthropology & Humanism* for publishing three of my short stories and to the Society for Humanistic Anthropology for awarding me the 2005 honorable mention in fiction. And thanks go to Susan Bright of Plain View Press for seeing this book through to publication. Most of all I am grateful to the people from Colonia Popular who became my friends and allowed me to enter their lives and record them for posterity.

Contents

Introduction: The Reality of Fiction

There exists a blurry border between fiction and creative nonfiction—the presentation of factual matter in a truthful way utilizing literary techniques such as scenes, dialogue, framing, and, debatably, internal monologue (Cheney, 2001: 226). John Steinbeck, who traveled with the dustbowl Okies to write *The Grapes of Wrath,* and Alejandro Morales whose *The Brick* People is based on his family's migration to and work on the Simons Brickyards in Los Angeles, both claim to be writing fiction. At the front of their books lies the typical and generic disclaimer that goes something like, "This novel is a work of fiction. Names, characters, places, and incidents are the product of the author's imagination or are used fictitiously. Any resemblance to actual persons living or dead, events, or locales is entirely coincidental." To Nayaran (1991: 141-142) this disclaimer constitutes a basic difference in *accountability* between fiction and ethnography, a non-fiction genre. Despite ethnographers' changing the names of people and places—in the interests of protecting their subjects—"an ethnography usually lets us know quite soon that the book is based on fieldwork among a particular people in a particular place at a particular time" (Nayaran, 1991: 142).

A central question for humanistic anthropology is whether the techniques of fiction (and the technique of fiction) are useful in portraying, representing, and/or evoking the lives of individuals embedded in a particular culture or subculture (including those of work, gender, generation, locale). In simpler and more general terms, can fiction throw light on the reality of human lives? And the answer is, of course it can. The concern of many anthropologists however, is whether presenting the human condition encountered and revealed in the field in fictional terms will erode the scientific claims of the discipline (e.g. Agar, 1990; Nayaran, 1999). This debate is ongoing.

A second question might be: What is fiction and what is not fiction? Creative or literary nonfiction canons hold that composite characters are fictional and that writers who create such characters are not writing any brand of nonfiction nor can ethically claim to do so (Gerard, 1996: 201; Cheney, 2001: 227). Yet many ethnographers present readers composite characters without perhaps realizing, and certainly not claiming or alerting the reader to the fact, that they have entered the realm of fiction.

The stories contained herein are about people I met, interviewed, and socialized with in a squatter settlement I call Colonia Popular, in Mexicali, on the U.S.-Mexican border. I lived in the *colonia* from 1988 to 1994, the first three years doing fieldwork and writing portions

of my Ph.D. dissertation (Wilson, 1992). In the course of fieldwork
I interviewed people about their migration and work histories,
accompanied some to their worksites (the municipal dump, the lettuce
fields of Salinas, the construction site that became Plaza Cachanilla),
and often worked alongside of them; to their places of recreation in
the *colonia* and nearby *colonias*, especially dances held on the occasion
of birthdays, *quinceañera* celebrations (a fifteen-year-old girl's coming
out party), or marriages—if not just for the heck of it; and to political
gatherings and demonstrations aimed at getting, first, running water,
and later a sewage system into Colonia Popular. Since 1994, I have
returned to the *colonia* several times a year, and Lilia, Socorro, Teresa,
and Jesús's Mamá have come to stay with me first, in Los Angeles, then
in the San Diego area over the years. These women have also taken part
in panels about women's work on the border and on squatter settlement
development that I organized for a Pacific Coast Council on Latin
American Studies and an Association of Borderlands Studies (part of the
Western Social Science Association) conference.

Colonia Popular is one of the poorest *colonias* in Mexicali and in
Mexico. Although people have replaced their initial cardboard houses
with more permanent materials, few enjoy the luxuries of more middle-
class households. Most now have a second-hand refrigerator and a
television, and bought these things soon after electricity was installed—
about two years after the *colonia* was established in 1983. A few were
unable to pay the costs the government demanded for this service, and
their houses remain without even a fan in the summer temperatures
that can reach 120 degrees Fahrenheit. Most of the parental generation
spent most of their lives working in the informal sector of the economy
as vendors, construction workers, garbage collectors or brickmakers, with
no pensions to look forward and no paid vacations. Many of the younger
generation has moved into work in the *maquiladoras* or one of the
industrial plants in the city, though not all have moved forward. I hope
that these stories will show how some of the poor struggle to make do,
and carve out an emotional, as well as material space in a world in which
they occupy the lower echelons of poverty. Their lives are filled with
friendships and relatives, however, despite daily struggles to put food on
the table and care for their offspring and aged or aging parents.

I wish I could claim the status of creative nonfiction for all of the
pieces, and for two of them ("The Rodina", "The Cartonero") I indeed
stuck completely to interviews, direct and overheard conversations, and/
or participant observation—though they are of course overlaid with my
point of view. But the most I can claim is that the stories are on the
borderline of nonfiction and fiction. They are not completely fiction

because they are based on real events in the lives of real people. They are not nonfiction because: 1) the dialogue I present is often not word-for-word as told me or observed by me ("The Presidente", "El Otro Lado"); 2) in one case ("Maquiladora Cousins") there is a composite character and the dates are slightly off; 3) things that happened over weeks, or months, are sometimes conflated into a few days or even one day ("La Presidente", "The Tablaroquero"); 4) sometimes people who were not present during a scene were added or people there were subtracted ("Maquiladora Cousins", "The Tablaroquero"); 5) in one story ("Maquiladora Cousins") I used internal monologue, a debatable practice in nonfiction.

Root and Steinberg (1991) call creative nonfiction—nonfiction using literary techniques—"the fourth genre." Perhaps there is a fifth genre that blurs fiction and non-fiction, similar to what Van Maanen (1988) described as "literary tales," a kind of writing that depends on long-term fieldwork and knowledge fostered by communication, empathy and friendship with people met in the field, a kind of writing which aims at portraying for the reader the struggles and small triumphs and joys of these people, a kind of writing which reflects the desire to give insight into the lives of people which cannot be achieved through other forms of writing; a kind of writing that focuses less on the personal experience of the writer and more on the personal experience of those the writer is writing about.

On the 2005 brochure for the Society for Humanistic Anthropology it is stated: "The Society for Humanistic Anthropology was founded in 1974 to open a dialogue on the various means by which anthropologists might evoke, represent, or give account of the human subject." On the pages of the Society's journal *Anthropology and Humanism* (formerly *Anthropology and Humanism Quarterly*) appear poetry and fictionalized accounts "from the field" that are published to achieve this goal. I hope my endeavors will be seen as humanistic because I focus on individual representatives of cultures and subcultures, and because my presentation is literary, however it may be flawed. I hope my endeavors will also be seen as anthropological because without fieldwork among the people portrayed—as well as the friendships that grew out of that fieldwork—I would never have come to empathize with these particular individuals, to know them, to become conscious of their problems, their hopes and dreams and philosophies of life, their idiosyncrasies and their routines, their work lives and the situations they needed to confront, often on a daily basis.

I am grateful to John Steward for his patience and aid in publishing my first story, "The Rodina," in *Anthropology and Humanism Quarterly*

(1992), Edith Turner and the judges of the 2005 ethnographic fiction competition for awarding me honorable mention for "La Presidente," the editors of *Anthropology and Humanism* for publishing my "Maquiladora Cousins," and Tim Hall, editor of *Struggle,* for having published my "The Cartonero" and "The Tablaroquero." And, of course, and most of all, I thank the people of Colonia Popular who became my friends and shared their lives with me.

In the end only the people I write about will know if I have captured the truth of their lives, or at least a partial truth of a portion of their lives. They have had proud moments in their lives, despite their economic poverty.

Only Chiapas? (1995)

I have seen the best minds of five generations   destroyed by poverty
struggling naked moaning sobbing howling in despair
fighting battles often lost   infants dying before one year
mothers fathers anemic shrunken crippled haggard hungering

Who dragged themselves through dusty streets at dawn   searched for a
way to survive   laborers for others   who had more   lands or capital
sellers   servants   shiners of shoes   bone pickers
great grandfathers   who rented clothes   from roadside stands
they hadn't even rags or cloth to spare   walked barefoot
queued up beside construction sites   mines   railroad lines
begged for a day's employment   at any wage
hawked *platanos* and mangoes   tomatoes and onions
while they did without   or did with less
offered   woven blankets   embroidered lengths of cloth   supplied by
middlemen   work of wives and daughters   straw hats   and mats   and
cane-backed chairs   *serapes*   *rebozos*   silver rings   and bracelets
carved statues   of dogs   cats   burros   children   saints   Madonnas
to people passing by   mostly tourists   from near by   far off   richer
lands   where exploitations had occurred   earlier in history   but now
were exported   mainly   not exclusively

Who sowed   hoed   cut   harvested   tended sheep cattle
horses goats   burros   on haciendas   from age seven   or eight
beside fathers   indebted by their fathers   at the hacienda store
cross-generational peonage   sweated in the sun
drenched in the rains   shoeless   bootless   illiterate
their mothers   sisters   daughters   worked free in the big house
washing   ironing   grinding corn   cooking meals they never shared
emptying slop jars and spittoons   sweeping floors and fountain adorned
patios amidst the bouganvilla   for the privilege to remain
indebted   without lands of their own   or any hope of any
until they revolted 80 years ago

Who after 16 years of civil strife after more than a million men had died
after dislocations unrepaired   after houses and scant possessions burned
after some murdered   after brothers lost   after daughters   sisters
mothers   wives   raped   and disappeared
some became *ejidatarios*   others *pequeño proprietarios*
some rural proletarians   owning little more than life
most flocked into state capitals   the Distrito Federal   U.S. border towns
some to sell their labor power in fluorescing factories   sweatshops
talleres   cantinas   on construction sites   and brickyards
some to vend *manzanas*   Marlboros   contraband radios   and *relojes*
to neighbors better off   Mickey Mouse hand puppets   ceramic
hamburgers slopping mayonnaise   rearing stallions made of stone
mixed with   traditional handicrafts   woven   dyed   embroidered
carved   painted   to visitors from nearby richer lands
some to cross the *raya*   to plant and harvest   crops in California
Arizona   Michigan   Oregon   Arkansas   Texas
or on the railroad lines
across the west   or in factories   foundries   sweatshops
in Gary   Chicago
Los Angeles   Detroit   San Antonio   until deported   when no longer
needed   60 years ago   40 years ago   20 years ago   today

Who then joined their urban cousins   some to live on lonely brickyards
no electricity   no fans   no refrigerators   no running water
no schools for their children   mold bricks to build the   malls   houses
hotels   industrial complexes   tourist complexes   banks
provide a subsidy   wrung from sweat of self   and family
to burgeoning urban conglomerations   inhabited by the dispossessed
and those parasitic on them

Some to invade   unused lands   to form   squatter settlements
shanty towns   *colonias paracaidistas*   *colonias perdidas*
colonias populares   to build   shacks   of tarpaulin   scrapwood
cardboard   crushed aluminum cans
trashed by Budweiser and Cola Cola
drinkers   to tap the holes   against the rain

Who arrived in greater numbers   after the Green Revolution
Rockefeller inspired   chemicals   fertilizers   monocropping
imported John Deere tractors   International Harvesters
the lucky buy land from the luckless   those whose crops failed   those
with nothing left to mortgage   most day laborers deprived of work on
farms now mechanized   no lands to sharecrop any more
machines replaced men   machines displaced men   imported machines
50 years ago   and today   and more tomorrow   now that Salinas has
revised and mangled   Article 27   for which the Zapatistas fought
in 1910   now that NAFTA reigns

Whose children labored beside them   from an early age
in icy mud   to mold the bricks   to mix the clay
toenails rotted   fungus growing   on ever damp   hands and feet
as ambulant vendors   selling tacos   fruit   vegetables   serapes
carved wooden statues   carved stone statues   white ceramic ducks
quartz pipes and bookends   silver earrings   hot dogs
as garbage pickers   collecting   metals   cardboard   bottles   for recycling
as itinerant construction workers   washers of windshields   on myriad
corners   singers on buses   jugglers   clowns   ice pick swallowers
shoeshine boys   dotting plazas   sometimes selling glue or *pingas*
newspaper boys amidst the traffic which sometimes grinds them down
anything for a spare coin   beggars without eyes   without legs

Who malnourished never obtained full growth   who poor could not pay
school fees   books   notebooks   pencils   crayons
though gradually there are more schools   unlike back on the *ranchos*
at least they learn to read   some of them   the young

Who built and build   Acapulco   Cancún   Cabo San Lucas   Mazatlán
Puerta Vallarta   Cuernavaca   tourist hotels   the Hyatt   the Hilton
the Westin   the Club Med   the Continental Plaza
the Fiesta Americana   World Trade Centers
conference halls for businessmen   and academics
shopping malls   Plaza Mexicana   Plaza del Sol   Plaza Cachanilla
Plaza Paradisio   hippodromes   country clubs   restaurants adorned
with Riviera murals   and hanging plants in multi-colored ceramic pots
places they cannot enter and enjoy   for lack of funds

lunch for one   at the Rosarito Beach Hotel   once a favorite haunt
of Hollywood stars   costs one day's minimum wage   no drink included
two beers at the Westin and the day's pay is gone
they build them   then return
to their *colonias perdidas*   their scrapwood dirt-floored shacks
since 40 years or more ago   until today

Who recycle   metals   cardboard   newspapers   collected in the local
dumps   to national   and multinational   companies
who gather   dented cans of food   thrown out   from newly established
supermarket chains   tomatoes   oranges   rotten on only one side
collected in the local dumps   fishheads for fishhead soup   thrown out by
the fish shop after filleting   clothing discarded by those so better off
they have no one to hand the garments down to   collected in the local
dumps   a fork   a spoon   a mattress   a broken chair   anything
of human use   found in the local dumps   up to now

Who rise early to make   tacos   burritos   tortas   to sell to factory
laborers   *maquildadora* workers   who made it through primary school
at least

Who sometimes cross to U.S. cities   to work   in Taco Bell   in
MacDonald's in Beverly Hills gardens   in L.A.   in N.Y.   in Miami
garment factories   Milwaukee   Chicago Pittsburgh   Detroit
foundries   in construction cleanup   carwashes   gas stations   as
janitors   bus boys   waiters   gardeners   maids
in old folks' homes   in rich folks' homes   in middle-class homes
in the countryside   to plant   cultivate   weed   prune   harvest
lettuce   apples   broccoli   oranges   peaches   tomatoes   grapes
melons   cabbage   onions   beets   lemons   still

Whose children will secure lots in squatter settlements
self-build housing   pay one third of infrastructural costs   in
installments   for electricity   for running water   for sewer systems
buy bricks   from the brickmakers   still living on   lonely   isolated
unserviced   brickyards   *their* children still the family's labor force
like that of the peasants from which they spring   their children   their
only welfare system

Whose growth   as those of parents   grandparents   is still stunted due
to lack of food   though not as much as previously   the population is
growing taller   and more can read   can write   can do their sums

Who will couple with daughters   of fathers like their own   see a movie
or two   Predator   Rocky III   Robocop   Superman   Batman
Pretty Woman   Deep Throat   Fantasia   Total Recall
dubbed in *español*   give them circuses if not bread
and the girls tint their hair yellow to look more like some Hollywood star
and spend their *maquiladora* savings   on mini-skirts   mascara   Clairol

Whose parents now have second hand   television sets   refrigerators
electric lights   if electricity has been extended to the newer settlements
local politicians sometimes support that now   listen to music from
radios   cassette players   even CD's   bought with a week's wages
at the local *tianguis*   or smuggled in when returning from
California fields   Wisconsin factories   Arkansas show horse
stables   dance in someone's lot   on Saturday nights   to celebrate
quinceañeras   baptisms   *bodas*   birthdays

Whose mothers gave birth without doctor's care   whose wives now go
to the Red Cross free clinic   or to the General Hospital   erected for
those who have no steady   formal sector job
the IMSS is overflowing anyway

Who will bring up children   less of whom will die before the age of five

Who are the only precious possession they still have   of which they
cannot be deprived   until later

Who will be unable to go to college   but may complete ninth grade now
it became a law in '95   at least those who can afford books   *cuadernos*
uniforms   shoes *cuotas* for new desks   new chairs   a roof
a real floor   take factory jobs   become cashiers   nurses aides
mechanics   bank tellers   if they study long enough
paid for the week

what is paid across the border for a day   that's why the multinationals
move there from the US   from Japan   from Korea   from Germany

Who hope their children will continue   the upward movement
their past   four generations   have described   for many
except those   who dropped   died   gave up   were killed in strife
along the way

Although now in the cities   there are more gangs   defending space
some of the *muchachos*   sniff glue   use that old *rancho* weed   inject
gobble down acids and pills   designed in laboratories on the other side
take a sniff of cocaine   on its way to the north
international exchange that keeps those in the *barrios*
on both sides of the border   unorganized   quiescent   stupefied
jobs last a few weeks   a few months   some cycled out so the company
need pay no benefits   and the factory managers   and the construction
engineers   and the supermarket supervisors   comply

And the peso has fallen just this year
multinationals arrive like carpetbaggers
the wage in dollars has been halved   prices have doubled
in the countryside   the Zapatistas unite

Little girl, Colonia Popular, 1991 (photo by author)

Child bathing, Colonia Popular, 1992 (photo by author)

Community center, Colonia Popular, 1992 (photo by author)

A Señora in Colonia Popular, 1994" (photo by author)

Girl standing behind water barrels in Colonia Popular, 1989" (Photo by author)

Doña Lolita's house, Colonia Popular, 1993 (photo by author)

Part 1:

Women

In

Colonia Popular

— *"The Rodina" is the story of a woman agricultural worker whom I came to know while doing Ph.D. research from 1988 to 1991 on patterns of migration to a Mexicali squatter settlement. The incidents in her life, as recounted in the story, are those she reported to me when I interviewed her in Colonia Popular, Mexicali, or which were revealed in subsequent conversations with her. "Lilia" (a pseudonym) invited to me to Salinas while she was cutting lettuce there, and took me to Watsonville to show me where she had previously lived, before and after meeting her current husband. I worked with her and other who appear in the story in the lettuce fields in the Salinas region for five days. All incidents in the story I witnessed first hand, or Lilia told me about; all the people in the story are real people. There are no composite characters.*

The Rodina

I

1991

She bent again to cut the lettuce with her nine-inch-long lettuce knife. First to her right, cutting the two parallel rows of lettuce planted on the same furrow, and setting the cut heads beside one another, in a double row. Then, in almost the same motion, shifting her weight from her right foot to her left, she cut the lettuce heads from the furrow on her left side and added them to the double row on her right side. She stepped forward, still bent down, cutting the rows of lettuce first to her right, then to her left.

There were other cutters about a hundred yards ahead of her, leaving her ever less to cut as she moved forward, but the cutter in front of her stayed the same distance ahead.

To her right a *muchacho* performed work in a mirror image of her own, cutting the two rows of lettuce first to his left, then the two rows to his right, shifting these last over to his left, forming them into a double row parallel to hers. To her left, two rows away, another *muchacho* worked, first cutting the two rows of lettuce to his left, lining them up in a double row then shifting to his right to cut those lettuce heads and placing them to his left, going through the same motions as the *muchacho* beside her. When he finished his section and she finished hers, two empty rows would separate them, leaving room for a truck to drive through the field while the cutters working beside the truck threw the harvested heads into 12 packing crates, six on each side of the vehicle, one cubic meter each. The crates rested on cargo palates; wooden if the lettuce was to be shipped overseas, cardboard if the lettuce was destined for points within the United States.

She finished her section rapidly, then walked past the *muchacho* working in front of her, checking to see she had left him another 10 yards or so to cut—not too much because you only rested while walking—and began cutting again, first to her right, then to her left. She cut cleanly, separating the head from its stalk and removing the overly mature dark green leaves, but not so close that any of the tightly bound light green leaves of the iceberg lettuce were damaged. Once in a while the out leaves of the harvested head were wilted, spotted light with brown. She chopped them off quickly with a skillful motion refined though her many seasons as a cutter.

The field was large, she had noted when they arrived at 5:30 a.m., and the lettuce was good. They would probably get 14 or 15 truckloads out of it. Since this was the first harvest of the field this season and all the lettuce was ready for cutting, it took just about an hour to get a truckload. Only her husband's quadrille, containing 16 cutters today instead of the usual 14, was working the field right now. Sometimes they had as many as 18 cutters in the quadrille when two or three of the *muchachos* at one of the motels would beg her husband, Ricardo, for a few days' or weeks' work, because they had to send money back to their wives who had just had babies, or to their mothers who were alone, or to a sick father, and he would add them to his list. Even if he had taken on more workers today, his quadrille couldn't have finished the field alone. If the supervisor didn't send another quadrille over to help them they would be cutting in this field part of tomorrow as well.

It was a pretty place, near the highway between Salinas and Watsonville. She looked around her as she stood up, her hands on the small of her back, stretching a moment to relive the pain in her lower back and thighs, as all the cutters did occasionally. She had only been picking for a week this season, and it took about two weeks for the body to become accustomed once again to the ceaseless bending, from left to right or from right to left, down the rows and rows of lettuce. She was strong though, even after having borne seven children, the last twin girls, now six years old.

Nine days ago she had left her children with her 19-year-old niece Marí, who had come back to Colonia Popular with her from Guanajuato. That was three years ago, soon after she received amnesty for having worked in the lettuce fields previously *sin papeles*, without documents. She, Lilia, had gone to visit her parents and her brothers and sisters and had brought Marí back with her to take care of the children. With Marí there she could work each season in Salinas. A few years ago she had gone on to work in Huron, too, but she wasn't going to do that this year. She wanted to be back in the *colonia* when the children began school again at the end of August, to make sure their school uniforms were ready and that they had money for books and notebooks. And she didn't like Huron. There were too many bars, too much drinking.

Marí's being there with the children also made it easier for her to commute with her husband to the lettuce fields in the Imperial Valley, where they cut lettuce in the winter. They had to leave the *colonia* about 3 a.m., to cross into Calexico in an hour and begin the drive to the fields a little before 5 o'clock. Marí didn't wake the children until long after Lilia

and Ricardo had left, since they didn't have to be in school until 7:00.
The twins had just started kindergarten last year. This year all would go
to school again. All but her eldest son, now 15. Almost 16, he insisted.
He wanted to work, he said. He wanted to work with them, cutting
lettuce. But he had no papers to cross and he was still so young, even
though there were *muchachos* his age, and some *sin papeles*, working in the
fields, she knew.

She had stayed in the *colonia* until the children finished the school
term so she could accompany them to the last day of parties given for
students and parents. The following day, when all the school festivities
were over, she had walked across the border to Calexico and boarded
a Greyhound bus for the 17-hour ride to Salinas, passing through Los
Angeles, then Santa Barbara, then King City and González on the way.

She made the trip alone, to join her husband, her brother Enrique,
and her brother-in-law Miguel, who were already living temporarily in
Salinas; her husband the foreman of a quadrille as he had been for
almost two years now, and the others picking lettuce in his work crew.
Once she crossed the border she was all right. It was crossing the border
alone on foot that scared her. When she crossed with her husband and
the other workers he brought to Calexico in the truck, when they worked
in the Imperial Valley, nothing had ever happened. They all showed
their Seasonal Agricultural Worker (SAW) amnesty cards, proving that
they were *Rodinos*, and the immigration officers waved them through.
But when she crossed the border alone, carrying her suitcase, explaining
that she was on her way to work in Salinas when they asked where she
was going, the immigration officials always stopped her and sent her to
customs. The women working there ran their hands over her, treated her
like a criminal, once made her undress.

Lilia finished her section, then walked across the several rows that
had been cut by the *muchachos*, heading toward the beginning of an
uncut row. She bent down and began cutting again after noticing that
her husband was using the van's walkie-talkie. He was probably calling
the *lonchera*, the circulating lunch truck, to come to the field. So they
would break soon, probably after she finished her first section on this
new row.

Her *cuñado* Miguel, her youngest sister's husband, came to work
beside her. He wondered if they would go back to the fields near
González tomorrow. Two years ago, when her husband had become
foreman for the first time, the company had given them an apartment
in González. That was the first time her *cuñado* had come to work so far
north with them, though he had worked for other companies in the

Salinas Valley. He liked González. He had stayed there with Lilia and Richardo.

But this year the company had given their foremen apartments in a complex in north Salinas. Not really *given*, since the company deducted $50 a week from her husband's salary. As a foreman he was paid $50 a day for selecting and picking up the cutters, driving them to the fields, making sure they learned the work, did not damage the lettuce, did not slack off, then driving them back to the two motels where most of them lived, seven or eight to a room meant for two or three or four, depending how many slept in the two beds, at $275 a week per room.

When she and her husband had first come to pick lettuce in Salinas for this company almost four years ago, when Ricardo was still a cutter, they had stayed in one of these motels too. Then it cost only $225 a week, but the cutters earned about $4 and hour, 50 cents less than now. Even working 50 hours a week one person couldn't make the rent. So eventually a cousin of her husband and a nephew of his and the nephew's wife, and another brother-in-law of hers moved in, and they took turns sleeping on the floor. They made their meals in the little kitchen, where there was only one frying pan to cook with. The manager never brought clean towels or sheets or toilet paper, she remembered. On their day off they took the towels and sheets to the laundromat, along with their clothes.

Miguel and Lilia agreed that they would probably move to another field tomorrow only if another quadrille came to help them with this one. They would work only four of five hours tomorrow if they had to return to this field. Her *cuñado* noted that the van wasn't working well, and joked that he hoped it would get them back to company headquarters so they could pick up their checks tonight, Friday. They should have good checks this week they agreed, since they had worked ten hours everyday except yesterday. The company never wanted you to work more than ten hours a day, because they would have to pay you overtime. You only got overtime on Sundays and then only if you had worked more than 45 hours total for the week. If you had worked less than 45 hours, you didn't get overtime even on Sunday until you had made up the difference. And there were days, especially during the end of the season, when you returned to the fields you had already harvested to cut a second time: the immature lettuce the cutters had left of the beginning of the season now ready for harvesting. Or sometimes you were sent back to finish a field you had begun the previous day when you had worked only four or five hours.

Thinking of the van, Lilia told her *cuñado* Miguel of the worst van the company had ever given them. Miguel hadn't been working with them then because they were cutting lettuce in the company's fields in the Imperial Valley and along the border in Arizona. He couldn't work that far south, because Immigration patrolled all around near the border and he didn't have papers. He could have qualified for amnesty, since he had been working in the fields in California for the past 11 or 12 years, but he didn't have the $185 filing fee and he was too shy to ask Lilia and Ricardo to lend it to him, and they hadn't known he needed it. So he only came to work with the company in their fields around Oxnard, Bakersfield, Salinas and Huron, farther north, past the second immigration checkpoints. Then he returned to Salvatierra, the *pueblo* in Guanajuato where both their families were from, when the harvesting moved south in the winter.

One morning Ricardo had been given a van with a really bad smell coming from the motor, Lilia told Miguel. It smelled like oil and rubber burning. Ricardo told the mechanic about it, but the supervisor told him to drive the quadrille to Yuma, to the fields a little more than an hour away, and the mechanic would go along in one of the semitrailers and fix it while the quadrille was working.

About half an hour east of El Centro the engine caught fire. They were afraid the van would explode, so after Ricardo pulled it to the side of the highway and they got the door open—it almost always stuck—everyone jumped out and ran some distance away while Ricardo and two of the *muchachos* doused the fire with drinking water from the ten-gallon cooler they brought to work each day. The motor wouldn't start after that, and there was no walkie-talkie in the van, so there they were, at 5:30 in the morning, standing beside the empty highway to Yuma. After awhile there was more traffic and two of the *muchachos* decided to hitchhike back to El Centro to try to get help.

A few minutes after they got a ride, at around 7:30, one of the semi-trailers belonging to the company came along and the driver, headed toward the fields near Yuma, spotted them and stopped. Ricardo told the driver what had happened, and he promised to get one of the mechanics, now in Yuma, to come back and help them.

It was almost three in the afternoon when the mechanic arrived in a pick-up. They had had trouble with one of the semis he explained. Working for almost two hours, he patched together the motor of the van, changed some of the rubber hoses, repaired it well enough so they could get the motor started again and drive back to company headquarters in El Centro—as long as they didn't go over 30 miles an hour.

The company paid each of them in the quadrille for four hours of work. But, Lilia complained, the quadrilles that made it to Yuma that days worked eight hours and were back in Calexico before 4:00

p.m., whereas they were beside the highway all day. Some of the *muchachos*–those who didn't bring their *lonche*, planning to buy it from the *lonchera*–were without food, though those who had shared their few tacos. And they had been without much drinking water left for the heat of the day. And they didn't get back to El Centro until 6 p.m.

Lilia and Miguel finished their section, moved up, walking between the furrows, ahead of the cutters in front of them, to begin another section. It was almost 10 a.m. The early morning mist had been burned off by the sun, and it was getting hot. Lilia took off her sweatshirt, tied it around her waist, adjusted her cap and the cloth beneath it that kept the sun off her neck, and bent again to cut the lettuce.

Less than half an hour later the *lonchera* turned north off the highway onto the dirt road first to the east of the field, then west along the northern boundary, then entered the harvested portion of the field and came to a stop near the van, which Ricardo had recently moved to where the lettuce had already been loaded so the drinking water and the portable bathroom attached to the back of the van would be nearer. Today it was Don Chuey again, Lilia noted to herself. Don Chuey followed the lettuce harvest from Bakersfield to Salinas, going to all the fields, even if they weren't lettuce fields, in the area. The foremen would call him up on his c.b. radio, using their walkie-talkies, and tell him where they were working, and he would drive to the fields. He and his wife made the tacos they sold for a dollar each and the *tortas* they made for two dollars each. They also sold sodas, many different flavors, in cans, for a dollar each. Then they collected the cans afterward and sold them to a supermarket, Lilia had heard.

The *muchachos* started moving toward the *lonchera*. Don Chuey gave Ricardo a soda, refusing payment, as he always did, even over Ricardo's protests. Ricardo never bought anything from Don Chuey because Don Chuey would never let him pay for it, partly because Ricardo was a foreman who called him rather than some other *lonchera* driver, and partly because they had known each other for many years, since Ricardo first came to work in the lettuce fields.

Lilia's brother Enrique went over to the *lonchera* to buy sodas for her, himself, and their *cuñado*. As usual Lilia had made lunch in the morning before they came to the fields. Today it was fried burritos containing the rice, beans, and chicken left over from their dinner the night before.

Lilia, Enrique, Miguel and Ricardo sat together in the field. The *muchachos* arranged themselves into small groups as well. The two brothers from Toluca, Mexico, sat with the three *muchachos* from the various *ranchos* in Jalisco who had crossed the border together with the same *coyote*, a smuggler of people without documents. They had stayed together ever since, working in the fields in Salinas and Monterrey county. The professor, who taught economics at the University of Guerrero except in the summers, when he came to work in the fields to supplement the small income professors earned, sat slightly apart from the two *muchachos* from Mexicali and the two brothers and their cousins from the *rancho* near Salvatierra where Lilia had gone swimming in the river as a child. The older man from Zacatecas and the man from El Salvador, who almost never spoke, sat on the fringes of this group as well, listening but not talking much.

Of the cutters, only Lilia, one of the boys from Mexicali, one of the boys from Jalisco, and the man from Zacatecas had papers. Richard had complained last night, when he was working with the list of names in his quadrille, how hard it was to get cutters with papers. No one with amnesty wanted to work in the fields anymore, he said. They could get steadier work for higher pay elsewhere.

Ricardo was supposed to fill out the papers for the company to have on file for Immigration, listing the identification each cutter in his quadrille had to prove his legal entry. He just gave a form to each of his workers and let them check off the identification they claimed to have. He didn't know how they did it. He could scarcely read English himself, and some of them didn't even know how to read in Spanish very well.

He never asked to look at the documents. He knew any documents they had would be false. Lilia's brother Enrique didn't have anything at all, not even a California identification card. They had to make up a social security number for him. He'd have to work under another name and another made-up social security number if he came back next year. By next cutting season in Salinas the tax office would have notified the company that no such social security number existed.

This was the first year Enrique had come to the United States, accompanying his *cuñado* Miguel. His car repair business in Salvatierra had failed, there was too much competition, he had debts to pay off, so he came.

Lilia looked at her *esposo*, her husband even if not by law, still handsome, though looking older than his 46 years. The sun had cut lines in his face. He was getting fatter now that he wasn't a cutter anymore. He had a green card, had had one for 19 years, since before they met. But he couldn't help her to get a green card because even though they had lived together almost 12 years, and had five children together, they were not legally married.

II

Lilia had come to the United States the first time 14 years ago, when she was 23. She came with a female cousin, crossed the border in the trunk of a car with her, joined another cousin and his wife in Watsonville. She had left her two little sons, one born only four months previously, with her mother in Salvatierra. Someone had to support them and her first husband, her legal husband, their father, wasn't interested in them anymore. He had left her a few weeks after the last baby was born, moving in with another woman, a woman he had had all though their marriage. Lilia left two weeks after the birth of his first child with that woman.

Her first job was caring for a dying woman who lived in a house on the road leading up to the hilltop apple orchards overlooking Watsonville. Ricardo was working for the owner of one of those apple orchards. One day when Lilia had taken the *señora* out to the front yard to get some sun, Ricardo drove by in the owner's pick-up truck, taking crates of apples down to the supermarkets in Watsonville and Castroville. He waved to her. After that, she waited to see him go by and they waved to one another. Then, one day, he came to talk to her.

He had been married before, to a Mexican-American woman older than he who could have no children and who died of cancer in her ovaries after helping him to get his green card. But Lilia was still married, by civil and church law, to her first husband, he whom she hoped never to see again.

When the elderly woman died, Lilia began living with Ricardo in his little shack on the apple orchard owner's property, beside the garage Ricardo had built for him of secondhand wood. Almost six months later she let herself become pregnant, as he wished. Her cousins no longer lived in Watsonville, and she and Ricardo did not have enough money for her to go to the local hospital, so a few months before their eldest son was born, he took her back to his *rancho* in Nayarit and left her with his mother. He returned to Watsonville, but came to see her two or three months each year for the next two years, leaving her pregnant each time. He wanted to see his own blood, he had told her when they began living together.

She wanted to be with him more often, though, and he with her. So after Ricardo began working as a lettuce and cabbage cutter, his old *patrón* having sold most of the apple orchards and retired, he brought Lilia and the children to Mexicali. They went to live with his sister and her family, but his sister didn't really want them there and let them know this with small discourtesies that became unbearable. So after a few months they looked for a house to rent. They found a room in a small *vecindad* beside a stream of water in a *colonia* with unpaved streets near the civic center.

And she and her five children—her first two sons who were not Ricardo's, the second three children who were—moved into the one room that was inundated with water every time in rained, the week or so it rained each year. She got to know her neighbors in the eight-room *vecindad:* the two sisters with their husbands and children, the elder widow with no one, the other three women and their families, one of whom rented two rooms because there were so many children. She lived there for another two years while Ricardo worked on the fields, wherever he could get work. He lived with them from December to March, when the lettuce and cabbage were ripe in the Imperial Valley, then moved north to follow the harvest. But he came back from the north every two or three weeks to visit them, to bring them money, so they saw each other more often, even during the months of the year he lived on the other side of the border. And she earned a little money selling the fruit-ades she made at home from syrups mixed with ice and water, sold them in front of the civic center, taking her children along, or leaving them with a neighbor.

Then one of the sisters told her an invasion was being planned, she had heard it on the radio, that a new *colonia* was going to be established, that they could all get a place to put a home of their own in an abandoned field on the edge of the city. The two sisters and their husbands and children, the widow who had no living family at all, and Lilia and her children took part in the invasion, arriving with a group of more than one hundred families late one evening, so the authorities would be met by an accomplished fact the next day. Each family pounded in stakes and strung plastic ribbon or twine from one stake to another to mark the boundaries between neighboring lots, and each set up a *ramada*—some slats of wood laid over four supporting stilts—to protect themselves from the burning sun.

All this happened while Ricardo was in Oxnard. By the time he returned to Mexicali and found out where Lilia was living from the neighbors who had chosen to stay in the *vecindad,* she had built a one-room shack of flattened cardboard cartons and scrap wood, covering it with a stretch of tarpaulin. Ricardo was pleased and the next time he returned to the *colonia* in a borrowed pickup truck and brought six wooded packing crates, broken down to their one-meter-squared sides and bottom. They built a better house, a house that has now become their storeroom, where Lilia washes clothes in the second-hand electric washing machine they later bought at a swap meet in Calexico.

There was no electricity in the new *colonia* for the first two years after the invasion, but they got along. To make a little money she bought ice and fruit syrups again and made *aguas* which she sold to others in the *colonia* or beside the highway where the brickmakers entered the dirt road leading to the brickyards.

The twins were born less than a year after she moved to the lot in Colonia Popular. When they were only a few months old her youngest sister and *cuñado* came to visit her. Lilia wanted to earn money to buy bricks to build a real house, with walls of yellow. So she left the children with her sister and crossed the border *sin papeles*—without documents—for the second time, this time with her *cuñado* Miguel, to join her husband in Bakersfield. She cut lettuce for the first time, in the same quadrille as her husband and *cuñado* for a different company than they work for now. For the next two years she crossed, *sin papeles*, to cut lettuce for a few months each year.

She was able to help buy the bricks and got her house with the yellow walls and glass windows, its large living room and kitchen separated by a bar—like in the apartments in Salinas—and two bedrooms and a real bathroom. And because she had crossed *de alambre*, jumping the chain link fence that separated Mexicali from Calexico, and worked without papers those years, she qualified for amnesty.

She kept working, each summer in Salinas, each winter in the Imperial Valley, to help make the house, the first real house she or her husband had ever owned, more beautiful. She wanted to buy a real sink for the kitchen and a real bathtub and toilet for the bathroom, for when piped water came to the *colonia*, perhaps in another year or two, *la presidente* of the *colonia*, Socorro, had predicted. And Lilia wanted to put bars on the windows, not because they were needed, but just because the ironwork was pretty.

III

The *muchachos* of Ricardo's quadrille ate their lunches quickly and returned to the rows of uncut lettuce. Lilia saw that Don Chuey had driven further up the dirt road, parked beside the cauliflower field: the cauliflower cutters were moving toward the *lonchera*.

She decided she would help load the next truck when it came, throwing the lettuce three or four at a time from the two double rows on each side of the truck into the packing crates, to rest her back a bit more. That was the way they all rested.

At 3 p.m. another quadrille came. The foreman was Raúl, Ricardo's nephew. Raúl's sister, Ricardo's niece, aged 14, who looked 12 or 13 but was listed on the work crew papers as 18, was working in that quadrille. Raúl had brought her up to live with his wife and children in Salinas after their parents had died several years ago. He and his wife had gotten amnesty *por tiempo*, for having been in the United States so long, since they had lived at times in Salinas, at times in Watsonville for many years, sometimes picking lettuce, sometimes strawberries, sometimes artichokes or cauliflower or apples. But his little sister did not have papers.

And Juanito was also in that quadrille; Juanito who had burned his back earlier this week on the exhaust pipe running up beside the cab of one of the semis when he had climbed up to see that the last lettuce heads were placed correctly in the crates. The company doctor had looked at the burn, said he was all right, and sent him back to work next day. The burn was still leaking. Lilia could see the dark spot spreading in an irregular pattern on the back of his shirt, darker than sweat.

She knew others in Raúl's quadrille, who had been in quadrilles with her before over these past three years, somewhere or another. One, Don Tonio, was from Colonia Popular too. He drank a lot and missed work a lot. No one wanted him in their quadrille. He had been in Ricardo's quadrille last year, but Ricardo had told him he already had too many workers when he asked Ricardo for a job this year. But Don Tonio and Raúl's wife's parents were *compadres*, from before the time Don Tonio had left his *rancho* in Nayarit. They were linked in ritual kinship from the birth of Don Tonio's eldest son, so Raúl couldn't refuse him. Even so, Raúl had told him that if he kept missing one or two days every week he would have to let him go, or he would get in trouble with the company.

And Don Emilio, who walked bent over from arthritis and from cutting lettuce for too many years. He should have been a foreman long ago. He could judge how many truckloads of lettuce were in a field within minutes of beginning work. And he was always right. But he had never learned to read or write, so he couldn't get a driver's license or keep the lists of quadrille members or time in and time out. He must be over 60, she thought, as she greeted him: "*Buenas tardes*, Don Emilio." He touched his cap to her with two of his fingers, a gesture of respect for her being a woman and the wife of a foreman, and a good cutter as well.

Lilia turned away and bent to cut the lettuce, first to her left, then to her right. They would finish this field today, then. Tonight, when they picked up their checks, the supervisor would tell Ricardo where to take them tomorrow.

"Resting" by loading lettuce, Salinas, 1991 (photo by author)

La Rodina, Salinas, 1991 (photo by author)

Cutting lettuce, Salinas, 1991 (photo by author)

This story received Honorable Mention for the 2005 ethnographic fiction competition held by the Society for Humanistic Anthropology. The original version appeared in *Anthropology and Humanism* (December, 2005)

— I was in close contact with "la Presidente" for six years, accompanied her to government offices to petition for services for the colonia, attended colonia meetings, and sat with her and "Teresa" over many cups of coffee, listening to their stories and discussions. We have also traveled to Los Angeles, San Diego, Corpus Christi, Phoenix, and Tijuana together and have been in touch for the 14 years after I moved from the colonia. I believe her sense of social responsibility is exemplary, if typical of many of the leaders of the colonias populares [squatter settlements] in Mexicali and elsewhere in Mexico.

La Presidente

I

The hot sun beat down, as it was accustomed to these months, presaging the 120 degree temperatures of summer, heating up the tin-roofed houses like ovens. Socorro wiped her kitchen sink with a rag whose origin had been a discarded shirt she found in the dump. She would go there when the afternoon sun began to move toward sunset, to look as usual for clothes for herself, her daughters, her three grandchildren. And whatever else of use she could find—perhaps even irregular diapers cast off by the factory for her newest granddaughter. Most of her forks and spoons were cast offs found in the dump. So were five of the mattresses on the six beds in the house. The dump was almost filled in, and no one knew where the new dump would open. Never as close as this one, just a half kilometer away.

She didn't need to look for anything for her husband any more. Xavier had left her for a neighboring woman and returned to Mexico City. From what she had heard from her daughter there, he was now driving a pirate cab. Her sons preferred to buy clothes at the *tianguis*, the open air market, with the money they earned.

Her only task today, or for this week, would be to go to the dump, wash and iron some of the clothes found there, and try to sell them door to door in the neighboring *Fraccionamiento*. She was no longer involved in *colonia* politics. Ever since Colonia Popular had been established, one year after they moved from Tijuana to Mexicali, seven years after they moved from Chihuahua to Baja California, nine years since they left Mexico City, she had been involved in something. It wasn't enough that she had helped her husband and eldest son, then 14, to build the house, first out of scrap wood and cardboard and aluminum cans, then over time with bricks and cement, and with the help of her two eldest daughters, sold newspapers and magazines and *novelas* from her husband's stall in downtown Mexicali in the mornings, but she had also been elected president of the *colonia*.

Socorro was glad that was all over now, the drawing up of petitions and carrying around notices of meetings from house to house, organizing the women in each tattered dwelling to go to the *Centro Cívico* and sit there in the cold corridors of one of the buildings, state or municipal or city, until some government official would hear their demands, or better, requests. Only her friend Teresa could always be dependent on to help her, rescheduling her work as a full time cardboard and metal recycler, to be by her side. Xavier only showed up during the bimonthly meetings, once held on the corner in front of the primary school in the colonia, more recently in the community building erected with the help of an NGO. And then he was often drunk and engaged in embarrassing harangues, as though he were a *político*.

The third year after they had invaded that empty stretch of land, filled only with broken glass, rotting carcasses or dried bones of cattle, and an occasional *guaje*, that parcel of abandoned earth which became Colonia Popular, she had been elected. Mainly because everyone was dissatisfied with the arrangements for getting electricity that the then president, the second one, had made. Chano, a factory foreman and thus among the better off of the *colonos*, had indeed organized all the meetings and demonstrations and petitionings to get electricity, and the meetings and demonstrations attended by representatives from each household. These were usually the women, since most of the men were bound to be out working somewhere during the hours the government offices were open. But the arrangement he had made satisfied nobody. Each family was to pay every month for the next year twice the amount a man earned working six days in a factory—just to get the electric posts and wiring extended to the colonia, and to each lot, but not including the electricity used each month. Part of the problem was that not too many men worked in factories. Or women. But even if they did, it would have been an overwhelming burden.

Most were brickmakers or garbage pickers or vendors like she and her husband had been, and as she, with the help of her youngest son, still was, now selling engine oil and fluid on the highway in front of the *colonia*. A number of young men worked in construction, or as mechanics helpers. The ones in construction sometimes earned more than the scattering of factory workers, the months they were employed. But they seldom worked more than 7 or 8 months a year. Some household heads could barely make it, even with their wives selling *tamales* or *pozole* on weekends, or cleaning houses in the better off colonias or running a *tiendita* to sell sodas and tortillas and some few canned goods to their neighbors. Most collected clothing for their families in the next door dump. The result was that some families had not been able to keep up payments for their lots. A few even got so far behind that they sold their small properties, then took part in one of the newer invasions with some money in their pockets to begin to pay off the lot there.

So she had been elected, and with much petitioning, gotten an extension to pay the electric fees over a three year period. It fell to her, as president, to make sure that each family got washing water as well.

As president she received the concession for the tanker truck from the municipal government, who also lent them the *pipa* as the water truck was known. Three times a week, their eldest son Everardo drove the *pipa* to deliver water from house to house, filling the barrels each family had placed in front of their lots. They charged, of course, but less than a commercial *pipa*, and the money earned barely paid for gas, oil, and repairing the occasional flat tire.

A couple of years after she was elected, then re-elected, president, and while the *colonia* under her leadership was petitioning the municipal government for running water to be extended to each of the lots, rumors began circulating. That she and Xavier were getting rich from having the *pipa*. That they didn't really want the *colonia* to have their own water system. That they had a bank account with millions of *pesos* in it. Rich from delivering water! Socorro mused angrily. They usually had to contribute money of their own to fix the *pipa* when it broke down or to change one of the six tires when it got a nail in it. Eventually they got the repair money back from the municipal government but often they went months waiting for the repayment and had to cut down to beans and tortillas and occasional fried egg until they were repaid.

And a bank account! How she wished she had one. If she had a bank account then maybe she could get a border crossing card and a *permiso* to visit her brother in Anaheim, California. They looked at things like that, the *migra* did, especially if you didn't have a job that paid *seguro*. They might reject you even with *seguro* or a bank account, but with neither one, forget it.

Shortly after than a new rumor took hold, started by Doña Cuca from the opposing faction. There were always opposing factions, to any president of any *colonia*, but this group seemed to be overwhelmingly filled with gossips and rumormongers. Doña Cuca had found out that Xavier had been born in Yucatán. "Yucatán" she had said, "That's down around Guatemala. They aren't even Mexican."

So some people from the opposing groups had gone down to the police station with Doña Cuca, and reported that she and Xavier were foreigners, *Centroamericanos*, probably living in Mexico illegally, and asked how the government could let foreigners run the *colonia*. Later that same week, a police car, blue and red lights flashing, pulled up in front of their house and waited until she came out. One of the policemen then handed her a summons. She had to go down to the police station with her birth certificate and Xavier's, proving she was born on a *rancho* in Chihuahua, and hoping that at least the police would know that Yucatán was a state in Mexico. They did, and all got a laugh out of it, but Socorro had to explain to a variety of people in the *colonia* why she had been called in by the police.

Then, early last year, she had taken part in the new invasion that established Colonia Unión across the highway. She and her *comadre* Consuelo and her best friend Teresa. They had all hoped to get lots for a son or a daughter. She had wanted one for Everardo, who was planning to marry soon. The problem was, someone had to be living there, staying every night until the papers were drawn up recognizing possessorship, or it could be repossessed. But Everardo was taking a class in technical drawing in the morning and since the piped water had been put in, working as a mechanic across town. So he couldn't stay there, gathering wood to cook for himself, walking more than two kilometers to catch the bus to school, then to work, then back again. She couldn't be absent from her house in Colonia Popular every night. Her husband just wouldn't allow it. He had told her so. And he wasn't willing to live there alone. Her daughters couldn't stay there. No one would leave girls alone at night. And her daughters were very pretty. The other boys were too young, and already in secondary school. They could only stay on weekends.

So, in the end, even though Teresa or her son Martín kept an eye on it for her, she lost the lot. Toward the end she was hardly ever able to get over to La Unión and another family, who owned nothing anywhere, just moved in, taking down the shack she had put up, with Teresa's and Martín's and Everardo's help, and replacing it with a larger one of their own. Using mostly her wood, she thought in annoyance, the wood she had painstakingly collected day after day over a period of weeks, from the dump. But she had to recognize the justice of it all. They had nothing. She, at least, had their house in Colonia Popular. Even if her husband had put it in his own name.

She thought of her husband: dynamic, dashing, handsome, proud of his Maya ancestors from the Yucatán. And unfaithful whenever he could be. She, on the other hand, had to ask him permission to leave the house. At least whenever he was in the *colonia*. Still, after twenty-three years of marriage. Even when she was organizing political meetings or going to demonstrations at the Civic Center. Xavier would let her go, finally. He was proud of her being president. But she would always have to give detailed explanations, almost beg. That meant she went out mostly when he was away. And usually Xavier was away. He spent the day at the stall downtown and some evenings he didn't come back until late. She didn't know where he was then, although sometimes, when he was drinking, he used to torment her with stories of women he had met in some bar or another downtown. And then, some months ago, he took off with their neighbor, the neighbor who for the past year always visited her in the early evening, the neighbor who she always served coffee, the neighbor whose children scampered in and out of her house, the neighbor she had thought was one of her best friends.

In a way it was hard. But in a way it was a relief. No more drunken scenes, no more being cursed at, no more being tormented, no more being ashamed of him in public. No more needing to ask permission to go out. But his leaving, he the father of their eight children, took something out of her. Perhaps it was the gossip that attended his departure, perhaps it was the ultimate gesture showing how little respect he had for her or their home.

Soon afterwards she lost the lot in La Unión. Just after the *Partido Revolucionario Institutional* was voted out. The new state governor was a *Panista*. She announced her retirement as president soon afterwards. All new officials had come into the state and municipal offices. She didn't know anyone anymore. She could have gotten to know them, but she didn't have the energy. And she was associated with the PRI, anyway. It was that party that had arranged for water to be put into Colonia Popular. In return for her promising them votes, of course. And they had lost the election. The first time they had lost in Baja California. There wasn't much purpose in being president anymore anyway. They had gotten the piped water.

Toward the end, Teresa had gotten sick, sick from cancer, sick for months, and it hadn't been fun anymore. Teresa wasn't able to accompany her all the time, like before. She lost her lot in La Unión too. Now Teresa was fine again, since the hysterectomy, but now it was all over.

II

While Socorro was musing, washing dishes in the tub which she filled from the faucet now on her lot, as almost everyone now did, at least if they had money for the down payment, then turning to start preparing the rice and chicken soup for dinner, she heard someone entering the lot.

"Hello there. What are you up to?" Teresa stood in the doorway.

"Come on in. Just making dinner. Would you like some coffee?" Socorro responded, pleased to see her *compañera*.

"You know me. I'm always ready for a cup." Teresa laughed, sitting near the door on one of the brown plastic chairs with its back pad missing.

After serving the coffee Socorro lit a cigarette, regretting Teresa no longer smoked. She had gotten a lung disease that had lasted almost a year. From working in the dump. Before she got uterine cancer. Better she didn't smoke, but it was one less thing to share. She offered her one anyway, knowing Teresa would refuse.

Teresa started the conversation: "Socorro. We got the water. We have to keep going."

Socorro replied: "You know we don't have contacts in the new government. The *Panistas* have all the power now. The only way we got water is because we knew the PRI people."

Teresa laughed, "And they knew us."

Socorro smiled, "We'd had enough demonstrations. Sat outside of their offices enough hours. Filled up their meeting halls to listen to some *politico* or other when they needed people for the television cameras."

Teresa said, "Well. Who knows what will happen next election. But we've got to start up again."

Socorro, knowing Teresa's boundless energy, the energy that had enabled her to get out of her sickbed when many thought she never would again, looked down at her cup, the outer edge cracked in one place, and said: "What's it now, Teresa?"

Teresa responded, "Don't be that way. You know the other faction is *totalmente* incompetent. All they can do is give dances on Saturday nights and attract the *borrachos*, the biggest drunks in the *colonia*. And most of the young people would rather go to the dances we gave anyway."

Socorro said shortly, not knowing what Teresa was getting at, "O.K. Teresa. What's up?"

Teresa took a sip of her coffee, looking Socorro in the eyes, before answering. "I was over to visit Juanita in La Unión. She knows some people in the municipal offices. She got to know them when they were petitioning for electricity. And they're going to get it. Soon."

Socorro looked up, doubtfully. "That's good. But what's it got to do with us? In this *colonia?*"

Teresa laughed, stretched out her hand to touch Socorro on the arm for a moment. "You know we've got to start organizing now. In another two years or so the water will be paid off. We've got to begin getting petitions together and making contacts to get the sewage system in. We've got to be *las viejas cabronas*, the old bitches, again. Starting now."

Socorro listened.

Teresa continued, "Lilia even brought a toilet and bathtub back from California when she and Ricardo returned from Salinas."

Socorro looked at Teresa. "That must have been expensive. And then we need to buy and lay down the pipes." Then, as an afterthought. "They're *Rodinos* so they can afford it."

Teresa replied, "But they're part of our *colonia*. And in the next couple of years we'll get together the money for pipes and shower fixtures and. . . . " "And the whole enchilada," she ended.

She finished her coffee and got up. "I've got to get some washing done. Come on over in the evening if you can get away. If not, I'll come talk some more tomorrow. After I make dinner." Before she walked out the door, she touched Socorro on the shoulder. "I'm not sick anymore. I'll be able to help you again. Just like old times. And, Socorro, *ninguna chingada madre*, not one damned person, can say you were getting rich from the *pipa* anymore. You were president when we got the chance for faucets to be put in."

When Teresa had gone, Socorro turned to cleaning the carrots and potatoes and chicken for that night's soup.

We did get water in the *colonia* while I was president, she thought. Now everyone who can afford the down payment has a faucet on their lots. And the others are saving up to get their own piped water, now that it's available. Let's hope that will be everybody.

I'm a *Priista*, she mused, but I didn't know anybody personally in the state or municipal governments when I began organizing the demonstrations for water. Me and Teresa. Teresa was always by my side, at every meeting and demonstration. Until last year, anyway. But now she's fine again.

III

In the end Socorro didn't agree to do anything. Her son Everardo *se juntó* soon afterwards, they didn't have the money for a real wedding so he and his *novia* just moved in together, and her daughter-in-law was pregnant within a month, so they had to start building a new room on the lot. Of course she helped collect the materials and nail together the walls and find a bed, going with Don Ramón and his wife Juliana to the new dump that had been opened twenty kilometers away several weeks before, just to see what she could find to furnish the room. Teresa and José didn't go anymore, now. Not since the problems in her lungs. Teresa had just started working in a glass factory. Her husband José had found a job as a watchman. Socorro could take off the afternoon hours from her stall on the highway because her youngest son just went to school in the mornings.

It was a couple of weeks after her fourth grandchild and first grandson was born and a few weeks after Christmas that the storm clouds began hovering over the city and the *colonia*, hanging above them intermittently for several days before they exploded into drenching rain drops. Rain always fell this time of year, never lasting more than three days, but even then turning the *colonia* into a muddy, slippery, slogging mess for about a week. Thick, ankle deep mire that caked on shoes, ruining them irremediably, and caused car transmission to erupt smoke and expire if their drivers tried to enter or exit from the *colonia*. Everyone got their feathers ruffled and it cut down on house to house visits, but everyone was used to it by now.

There was a lot of thunder in the middle of the night this time, which made Socorro sit straight up in bed a couple of times, thinking a drunken intruder had entered the kitchen and was tossing around pots and pans or that the laminated tin roof over Everardo's new room had fallen off and landed on the pile of bricks, bought for the new addition to the house, optimistically stashed outside.

It got worse. The rain continued. The brickmakers and cardboard collectors and ambulant vendors and even the fixed vendors with stalls open to the weather, weren't able to work. Many of the brickmakers who hadn't gotten around to firing before the rains came lost weeks of already molded bricks. Such things happened every year. But this time it kept raining. After five days of rain it was almost impossible to get around the *colonia*. Feet sank inches deep, shoes and even boots were sucked off by the deepening mud, small lakes separated neighbors who lived across the streets from one another. The buses that transported the several girls who worked in the *maquiladora* plants could not enter.

The rain kept falling. No one had been able to wash clothes for a week. More and more people were out of drinking water. The water truck that sold five gallon plastic bottles of drinking water could not drive in through the sodden, muddy roads. Those *colonos* who had faucets began boiling that water to drink and cook with, hoping the chemicals in it wouldn't kill them. Their less fortunate neighbors, those who hadn't paid to have the water pipes extended to their lots, sent children struggling over with buckets to take home the tap water. The stores in the *colonia* closed down because the tortilla man and the Coca Cola and Pan Bimbo trucks and the fruit and meat vendors hadn't been able to get through the mud and even the tiny *tienditas* run by housewives weren't offering as much because their owners hadn't been able to carry the huge bag loads of goods from downtown or from the supermarket to restock them. You could hardly walk without slipping and falling, while carrying little more than yourself.

News came over the television about the situation in Tijuana. Houses in El Tecalote and Colonia Obrera and El Florido and other *colonias* populated by the poor began sliding down the hills. First six people had been found dead, then fifteen. Others might be buried beneath mud slides. The government sent soldiers in to relocate people; they feared the Rodriguez Dam would overflow or burst. Ten thousand people would have to be evacuated. Socorro watched. Others in Colonia Popular watched. They watched until their electricity gave out due to the rain.

In the *colonias populares* in Mexicali, where no houses were built on hills, for there were no hills, the house with dirt floors became houses with mud floors punctuated with small but growing puddles. Water crept in even where people had cement floors. Pieces of roofs began to give way in the poorest structures. Buckets were set under leaks and emptied frequently into the growing ponds surrounding wooden or cement-block or brick or adobe or scrap wood and carton residences.

Somehow Teresa made it over to Socorro's, entering her door covered with patches of mud on her knees and shins and chest and elbows and forearms and sticking on her chin and in her steel grey hair. She had slipped and slid and fallen at least twice on her three block walk. This time she was angry, initially saying very little, sitting in the white plastic covered armchair with one arm missing, while Socorro stood in the puddle in front of the stove, waiting for the tap water to boil for coffee, arms folded across her chest, with the cuffs of her shapeless grey sweater hooked around her thumbs.

Finally, when Socorro filled the two cups with boiling water and brought them over to the ancient sideboard she used as a kitchen table (found in the dump—a discard from the house of someone whose roof was not leaking), Teresa spoke. "You know María's house has collapsed." María lived on the street behind Teresa's in a one room shack made of scrap wood and cardboard, covered over with orange and blue sections of tarpaulin.

"No," Socorro replied. "I haven't left the house for the past couple of days. Juliana told me my *comadre* Consuelo's roof is leaking in the bedroom and may fall in."

"Everyone has water in their houses," Teresa snapped. "We can't even walk without getting our feet soaked. I'm up to my shoe tops in mud even when I cook. I just thank the *Virgén* that we have a real floor in the bedroom."

Socorro looked at her growing puddles, took a sip of her coffee, waited.

"You know La Mirimba isn't going to do anything," Teresa continued, calling the current president by her nickname. "She just wanted to be president because her sons are in and out of trouble with the law and she has hopes of being able to do something if one of them lands in jail." And then, laughing, "And because she likes to dance. *Hijóle* can she dance."

Socorro smiled, remembering how "La Mirimba" had gotten her name, took another sip of coffee.

"Do you know what they're doing in La Unión?" Teresa asked and when Socorro looked at her expectantly she continued. "The university is getting the government to bring in truckloads of sand and pebbles to dump on the roads so the people and trucks and *quién sabe cuánta madre*, who knows what other stuff, can get in and out."

"Yes. I heard it on the radio. And Juanita told me something about it." Socorro knew that one of the professors was a friend of the organizers who had established and ran La Unión. Juanita, the president of La Unión, had introduced her to him once. "They're worse off than we are. They're almost two kilometers from the highway. We're only half a kilometer away. They haven't had drinking water since two days after the rains began, and the *pipa* hasn't been able to get in either so they're living on rain water," Socorro added defensively.

"And they have over two thousand families living there and in the amplification, and we have less than two hundred. So the government's not going to do anything for us. No truckloads of sand and pebbles for us folk," Teresa said, then drained her cup. "Unless we go and ask them to do something, the *hijos de sus chingadas. . . . .*"

Socorro got up and filled her cup and Teresa's with more boiling water, waited while Teresa stirred in the Nescafé and sugar. "That's the president's job," she said finally.

Teresa tasted her coffee, added some more sugar. "You know La Mirimba. Doesn't know what to do. She just knows how to organize dances. And not even that recently. There hasn't been a dance in the *colonia* for the past six months. Who knows what she did with the money she got from them. I don't see anything being done here in the *colonia*. She's never been able to organize anybody to do anything. Except drink beer on Saturday nights. And that my Don José and I can do alone, thank you."

Socorro got up and threw a bucket full of water out into the yard, put it back under the leak near the refrigerator. María and Consuelo were hurting. The brickmakers and garbage pickers and vendors—the majority of the people in the *colonia*—were hurting. They would hurt less if trucks, with water and other supplies could get in and out. If they could drive out of the *colonia* to a supermarket to buy those things that not even the *tienditas* brought in. Not that they were able to bring anything in. Or drive out to do other chores. That meant getting the government to spread sand and pebbles on the *colonia's* dirt roads, now mud roads, though. She looked out an opening in the wall at the growing ponds in front of the houses, the expanding morass separating her house and Consuelo's.

Then, she turned back to Teresa. "I've got to try to go to the grocery store today. We're out of beans. I was going to send my *chamaco*" she said, referring to her youngest son. "But I might as well go myself. If we can make it though the mud to the highway, to the bus stop. I'll go to the supermarket near the *Centro Cívico*. But first we'll go over to the municipal offices. We can probably get my *comadre* Consuelo and some of her daughters and Juliana and Lilia and Lucia and María to go along. And anyone else who wants to go can come along too." She added, smiling, "Slipping and sliding out of here."

Teresa laughed, slapped her thigh. "Covered with *pinche* mud up to our foreheads."

New Invasion, 1990" (photo by author)

The original version first appeared in
Anthropology and Humanism, 2003, Vol. 27, No. 2:
pp. 185-191.

*— This is a short story about four young women who
went to work in the Mexicali foreign-owned assembly
plants (maquiladoras), told from the point of view of
one of them. Two are composite characters; all live in
the colonia (neighborhood), I call "Colonia Popular."
Their stories are not untypical of the young maquiladora
workers along the northern Mexican border. The
phenomenon of relatives networking each other into
worksites is also common. Despite the examples of
unhappy marriages and abusive men surrounding them,
the young women in the colonia still hope one day to
find a true love, a responsible man who will give them
affection and take care of them.*

Maquiladora Cousins

I

December 1995

Ay caramba, I sit here in front of my microscope, carefully soldering a
tiny orange square onto what I now know is a circuit board. I am unsure
if their piece is destined for a VCR, a television, or a computer. All these
things are assembled in the factory where I work, where they change
us around from time to time so we don't get too friendly with the girls
on the line beside us. "Work and not talk," is what our line manager
tells us. I've heard it daily all the time I've worked here—almost a year—
sometimes directed at me, sometimes at one of the other *muchachas.* The
line manager is tall, lanky, shirt slouching out of the back of his pants,
pale red moustache contrasting with his coffee-colored hair. He stares
at my legs, sometimes touches my shoulder, sometimes pulls a lock of
my long black hair, sometimes lets his hand slip to feel my breast, then
laughs when I jerk away and look at him in anger. *Híjole,* I am not the
only one he treats this way. Some of my coworkers know how to take it as
a joke, part of the hazards of the workplace. He's married anyway, with
four children, they say, *cabrón* that he is. But the bus driver who takes
us to and from work, circulating through all of the *colonias populares* on
the south side of Mexicali, is married too. That doesn't stop him from
flirting with my cousin Ana, and even asking her out.

My cousin Ana works here too. We both applied at the same time,
urged on by my Mamá, who heard from my cousins Estela and Laura that
there were work openings. Both Estela and Laura work here as well. We
all live in Colonia Popular, but Laura and Estela live with their widowed
father, my mother's brother Matias; and Ana, since her mother died of
uterine cancer, lives with us—me, my Mamá, and my younger sister. Laura
and Estela's mother died of cancer too. *Híjole,* there are rumors that the
barrels we used to hold water for washing ourselves and our dishes and
our clothes came from the chemical companies. And that the chemical
residues cause cancer. We stopped using the barrels several years ago after
the city finally gave us water faucets on each lot. After many petitionings
and demonstrations organized by Doña Socorro, *la presidente.* No need
anymore to buy water from the circulating water trucks, not even the one
driven by Doña Socorro's eldest son. But for some people, I guess, it was
too late.

My mother's house used to be full. The bodies of my brothers and sisters and at times my Uncle Gilberto and my cousins were strewn all around the bed-sitting room and the kitchen at night, most of us on mattresses we retrieved from the dump. The concrete floor my Mamá eventually put in was harder than the dirt floor we used to have, but at least the ants aren't all over the house anymore. I have five brothers and seven sisters, but almost all are married now and have moved out. My eldest two brothers and one sister had married before I was born. But they always come around to visit—my sister all the way from Mexico City.

Púes, it was because my other brothers, the younger ones, married and moved out that I, and Ana, came to this electronics plant. Although they promised to help my Mamá, they soon had babies to support. Then they both got lots in the new *colonia*, La Unión, and had to buy building materials and all the stuff you need for a house, and plates and pans. Their houses are still just made of scrap wood, holes stuffed with aluminum cans or pieces of tarpaulin, or even plastic bags, like we used to have. But they have cement blocks now, to make their houses better someday. Then, too, neither one is employed full-time, but just goes from one job to another as it comes up—a few months in the carrot-packaging plant each year, maybe loading trucks for a few weeks, a few months in a car repair shop, or whatever else they can get. Only my eldest brother, Luís, who is a building contractor, has something like a steady job, and there are slumps for him too. Sometimes he can't find jobs in Mexicali and has to go to Rosarito or San Luís Río Colorado, and once he even took his crew to Guadalajara to work on a hotel. He used to give work to my other brothers from time to time, but they'd get into fights, mostly over how much he paid them, so they all went their own ways. In any case, after my other brothers married they couldn't keep helping out my Mamá so much. Luís does always try to help out. He bought my Mamá her first pair of eyeglasses when she turned 55. *Hijole*, she'd been going around half blind most of her life, believing the blurred images she saw was what everyone say. We became aware she had bad eyes after Luís got us a second-hand television set from Virreyes, that great big *tianguis* on the edge of the city, where most of the families in the *colonia* go shopping for their household needs. My Mamá couldn't follow the *novelas* because she couldn't see who was who. So Luís took her to an eye doctor and got her glasses. But Luís can only do so much. He has four daughters now and a very demanding wife.

Ana and I had enrolled in a bilingual secretarial course after finishing secondary school. My stepfather was still giving money to my Mamá, even though they weren't living together anymore. It was for my youngest sister. She's his only child with my Mamá. He stopped sending money about a year ago, shortly after he moved another woman into his house, a couple of streets over from us. *Cabrón* that he is. Luís was giving more than he does now, too. There's less work for him since the peso fell in 1994. Many of the people who would have given him work went bankrupt, he told us. They didn't have enough dollars to buy the building materials imported from across the border.

My Mamá earned her coins reselling ceramic figurines from door to door in the *colonias*, and by collecting clothes from the dump. Our *colonia* was right beside the municipal dump until it got filled up two years ago, and they moved it to an *ejido*, communally held land, more than 20 kilometers away. Lots of housewives—and even men—collected discarded clothes, utensils, furniture, even the dented cans of food and the fresh fruits and vegetables with only tiny rotten spots that the supermarket chains dispose of in the dump. Ana and I often helped my Mamá collect stuff. Then we washed the clothing in the second-hand washing machine Luís gave to my Mamá one Mother's Day and hung them to dry on the clotheslines running in front of our house. We would all work washing the clothes, me, Ana, and my younger sister, feeding them into the faded yellow wringer after we washed them, draining the water into buckets, then filling up the machine with the hose attached to our lot's faucet, then rinsing them and feeding them through the wringer again. *Ay caramba*, machine load after machine load, as the old thing rocked on its legs when the agitator went into its back and forth motion. But it was a lot easier than when we washed everything by hand. Some of the clothes we kept for ourselves, but most my Mamá packed up into the large carton boxes she had found in the dump. Then Luís drove them over to the bus station and sent them to my sister who lives in the Federal District, Mexico City. She sold them as second-hand clothing in the open air market there—a market they say runs almost two kilometers long and four or five streets wide and is called *Tepito*. Then, when she came to visit, usually once a year during the summer, when her kids weren't in school, she brought half of the money she had earned to my Mamá. Now my Mamá can't do that anymore, since the dump was filled in here beside us, and dirt was spread over it by the city.

It was almost two years ago, too, that my brothers got married and moved out. They didn't really get married in Church or anything. They just moved in with their women, decided to share a separate roof with them. And that's about the time they closed the dump near us. So, for one reason or another there was less money coming in. Or my brothers were moving out, or my stepfather stopped sending money, or there was a peso devaluation, or the dump closed down. So my Mamá suggested we ask my cousins Lorena and Estela if they could introduce us to the

plant manager, see if there were openings. At first Ana and I tried to
keep on with our studies and work at the same time. But then, *hijole*, we
had household chores when we were home, having to serve our brothers
when they came to visit, having to wash our clothes, having to help my
Mamá put price labels on the ceramics—little things. My Mamá felt that
if we had a good paying job, why did we have to study for another? She
pointed our that she had never learned to read or write, but still earned
her few *centavos*. In any case, there was no money for next year's tuition.
Ana's father, my Uncle Gilberto, had lost his job in the furniture factory
in Calexico after the Immigration caught him using his visitor's pass to
cross to work, so even Ana had no way to continue the secretarial course.
My Mamá was concerned how to pay for my youngest sister's notebooks
and pens and pencils and crayons and the monthly school dues in the
primary school now that my stepfather had stopped sending money.
There was no one to help with this except Ana and me, and Luís when
he got contracted. So Ana and I dropped out of the secretarial course. I
guess that was our destiny.

II

July 1996

Ay caramba, I'm walking down the muddy, rutted street, trying to
avoid the puddles that formed with the surprise rain a few days ago. I'm
walking to where the factory transport picks us up. I board the bus this
week with only my cousin Estela. We drive past the new *colonias* that have
sprung up since we moved to Colonia Popular, take a right just before
the Pemex station, then another right to drive up the road that goes to
San Luís Río Colorado, passing many factories and packaging plants on
the way before we get to our *maquiladoras*. It is very hot, as is usual during
Mexicali summers, and the bus feels like a *chinche* oven. The heat causes
haze to rise up over the potholed highway.

It's just Estela and me today. Before, Lorena and Ana had been with
us and the bus trip was more fun. *Híjole*, we had our own little family
group. Ana stopped working several months ago not long after she
became sure she was pregnant. The father was the night-shift bus driver,
a married man with three children. The same one that was always flirting
with her, talking about taking her out, then hanging around our house.
Once he found out she was pregnant, he never came around again,
cabrón that he is. He still has the same job though, driving the bus for

the factory workers. Although I tried to advise Ana against seeing him, my Mamá didn't. Maybe she thought Ana was her revenge for her own failed marriages, both with my last stepfather and with her real husband. Although my Mamá has lived with and had children with four different men, she was only legally married to one. He was the father of eight of my brothers and sisters, though not of my eldest brother, or of us, the youngest ones. My Mamá left him when he wouldn't stop running around on her. He had various mistresses, and children with one, and probably even more one-night stands over the 12 years he and my Mamá spent together, *cabrón* that he is. She left him, back in Mexico City. She'd gone to Mexico City from the small town in the state of Jalisco where she was born, to work as a house servant. She was then a teenager pregnant with my eldest brother. Her husband-to-be was a baker who lived down the street from the house she cleaned. Her *patrona* sent her there daily to buy sweet cakes for breakfast. So they met, and flirted, and courted, and married. But, *híjole*, he turned our to be one who flirted with many women and courted them. After enduring years of humiliation at the hands of her husband, which she sometimes cries with rage about, my Mamá left him and came north to Mexicali, where we live now. Here, one of my uncles was living, Gilberto, Ana's father. My Mamá went to work in a bar to support the youngest ones that she'd brought with her, she says. There she met my father. I don't remember him, although he was around until I was two or three years old. Then he crossed the border into the United States and we never heard from him again. Sometimes, when we have visits and my Mamá takes a drink of brandy *Presidente*, she tells us these stories about her life. And some of her life I do remember.

I remember best my last stepfather. He was with us from a couple of years after Colonia Popular began in 1983 until little more than three years ago. He and my Mamá each got their lots in the *colonia*, but he lived with my Mamá on her lot. *Ay caramba*, my Mamá often fought with him because he was always criticizing my brothers, the ones who still lived at home, expecting them to help him out for free in his car repair shop, nagging at them about how much they ate and how little they did. And he'd drink a lot sometimes and get nasty—*Ay chihuahua*—with my poor mother who has not had a good life. Then my last stepfather and my Mamá started living apart. He kept sending money for my youngest sister, though, and my Mamá did his laundry and sent him meals in return. And some nights they'd stay together. Then he moved another woman in. *Ay caramba*, my Mamá said she was going to go and haul her out of his house by her hair. Several times she said that. She said it to us, and to the neighbors down the street, and to *Doña* Socorro, her *comadre*. But she never did. She just decided that it was over and no great loss. Except for the money.

It was kind of tit for tat. My mother's husbands had been unfaithful to her, so it didn't matter if her niece became the mistress of a married man. "He earns good money, doesn't he?" she once asked, as a kind of explanation for why it was all right that he could afford a mistress, that his wife and children would not suffer, would not starve. I even think my Mamá hoped he'd leave his wife and marry Ana. He used to bring up bagfuls of groceries when he came to visit Ana, and he'd stay overnight. Big bags filled with stuff we almost never saw anymore. Ham, fresh cheese, grilling beef. Sometimes ice cream. Sacks of beans and rice and flour.

After some months into her pregnancy, Ana, with her real bad morning sickness, decided to quit her job. She should have told him first, before quitting. He teased her about getting fat, but for some reason she didn't want to tell him she was carrying his child. Maybe she knew he'd take off. When she finally told him, he never came back, *cabrón* that he is. No more visits once or twice a week, no more holding hands with Ana when they went to the local store to buy tortillas or milk for my Mamá. I wonder if any man can be trusted. One always hopes—I know from my Mamá and sisters and cousins—that one will find a good man to marry. But sometimes it is not one's destiny.

Of our family only my cousin Estela still works at the assembly plant. She started about a year after her baby was born, shortly before her mother—my aunt—died. She'd had a *novio*, a sweetheart, she loved a lot, but when his family decided to return to their rancho in Jalisco, he left without inviting her to come along. So she sort of rebounded and took up with a widower who promised to marry her. But he drank a lot and never had a steady job. Sometimes he worked on one of the brickyards, making bricks for a piece rate. But then he'd go on a binge and lose his job. They say he went back to Sinaloa because a brother of his died. He never did come back here to Mexicali. He left Estela pregnant, though, and about a year after her little son was born, she looked for a job to support herself and the baby, even though she still lived at home. My uncle Matias's job as a night watchman didn't pay enough for her to buy clothes and toys for the baby. He was barely making it and depended on Laura's husband to bring food into the house and pay the electricity and water bills.

Laura, Estela's sister, left the *maquiladora* shortly after her husband found a relatively steady job loading trucks for the Coca Cola plant. He had worked for my brother Luís for some years and even for a couple of years after he married Laura. But he had a strong personality and fought with Luís because he wasn't paying all his workers' medical insurance, which they are entitled to, by the way. He was unemployed for a while, or just got jobs by the day or by the week, and he started sniffing glue and smoking marijuana again, things he'd promised Laura he wouldn't do once they became *novios*, sweethearts. One day Estela came home—they all live on my uncle Matias's lot—and told Laura they were looking for workers at the plant. So Laura went along with her the next day, lied and said she was single and had no children—although she already had two—and readily admitted to the personnel interviewers that she was on birth control pills, something they made all their female workers promise they were on. *Hijole*, she couldn't get medical insurance for the children because she lied, but at least she was earning enough so she could buy them food. Her husband couldn't say much since he had no steady work, but before Laura started working he was always complaining about there never being any meat in the meals. "Now you'll get meat," Laura told him.

After he found work loading trucks, though, he made her quit. When my uncle Matias asked him why he didn't let her go on working for a while longer, so they could get ahead, he said, "*Púes*, I'm a jealous man. I don't want her working with strange men." Maybe he was afraid she'd meet someone nicer at the factory, more steady. He still sniffs glue and smokes marijuana with his friends on the corner. Some of his friends do even heavier stuff. I'm sort of surprised my uncle asked Laura's husband why he didn't let her keep on working. He never let his wife—mi *tía política*, my aunt by marriage—work outside of the house either. She even had to argue for some months before he let her sell sodas and sandwiches to the school children from the house. They live across from the primary school. He always thought only men should bring in a wage. He let Elena work, though. But Elena was his disappointment. *Ay chihuahua*, she had a baby but not a husband. And also, maybe there were just getting to be too many grandchildren. Or maybe he thought he just couldn't rely on Laura's husband and couldn't go it alone anymore, after my aunt's death. He still mourns her deeply, sitting in a chair on their lot, where they used to sit together. Now he drinks more and just stares into space. And now Laura's husband was fired from his truck loading job and is recycling cardboard and metals from the dump. But he won't let her go back to work.

Anyway, it's just Estela and me now, from our large extended family. I'd like to leave too. *Hijole*, at time my back aches so that I can't find a comfortable position to sleep in at night. I just keep my youngest sister awake as I toss around on the old mattress we share, trying to find a way to take away the aching. And my eyes are becoming more and more blurry from looking through the microscope. At times they don't clear up until several hours after I leave the plant.

III

May 1998

Well, the line manager isn't staring at my legs and touching me anymore, *cabrón* that he is. They say the general manager sent him to one of the company's other plants. The new line manager is younger, single, but more serious, even sort of shy. And Ana has a boyfriend now who lives across the street to houses down and was always looking at her when we had dances in the *colonia*. Most of the time he's in the United States picking lettuce in Salinas or Gonzalez, and sometimes right across the border in the Imperial Valley. But wherever he's working, he always comes back to the *colonia* with gifts for Ana and the baby and gives her some money so she doesn't have to work. She's his wife in a way, although they still don't live together. He mostly stays with us when he's here, though. She's wondering whether, if she has his baby, he might take her to live across the border with him.

Laura is thinking of going back to work even if her husband doesn't want her to. He has started smoking crack with his friends on the corner and is beginning to miss work at least once every two weeks. She doesn't know how long it will be until they fire him. But she knows that if he doesn't straighten up, they eventually will.

Estela keeps on working but has changed assembly plants. She wanted to rest for a couple of months and be with her little son, so she did. Her eyes were getting blurry too. She hated electronics assembly so much that she went to work in the car accessories plant. There are a lot more men line operators there. Laura and I are hoping she'll meet someone nice.

There's something new in my life, though it has its history. I'll be getting married soon. I've known Francisco for several years now. He's one of my brother Luís's construction workers. I first met him at a party at Luís's house. Luís always gives his workers a party after they finish a construction job, tells them to bring their girlfriends, and of course invites the family. Francisco was very nice to my Mamá and to us. And he didn't invite a girlfriend. He's rather shy, but very courteous, like the people recently arrived from the *ranchos* in Jalisco, where my Mamá was born. He didn't dance with anyone at the other dances in the *colonia*, but he seemed to be around Luís's house whenever I went over to visit my brother or to take him some *tamales* or *enchiladas* or something special my Mamá had made. Then, *híjole*, Luís began bringing Francisco over to our house. Then, one day, at a dance in the *colonia*, Francisco asked me to dance. We danced several dances that night, and he didn't dance with anyone else. Since then he's begun coming around to the house even without Luís. My Mamá likes him and sometimes invites him to stay for dinner. Sometimes we watch *novelas* together. And at night we go out to talk on the corner of my Mamá's lot, then he kisses me good-bye before he leaves. Sometimes I get many kisses. But I don't let it go beyond that. I don't want to end up like Ana and Estela. Nor does he push me. He respects my decisions.

Francisco is a drywaller, so he gets good wages. Luís promised to pay his medical insurance if we get married. Francisco doesn't use drugs and he doesn't drink more than a couple of beers at a time. My first stepfather used to get *so* drunk on weekends, and one of my brothers drinks too much too. It's such a waste of money, and then there are always fights. Since Francisco doesn't use drugs, I won't have Laura's problem—a husband constantly doped up on something. And he doesn't seem to be a *mujeriego*, a woman chaser, so I won't have the problem my mother had with her legal husband. Even though Francisco has had a *novia* or two before me, it was nothing serious, he says. I'm the first he wanted to marry and have children with, he says, and I just hope I'll be the last as well. Maybe he'll be like Luís—responsible, faithful, and loving to his wife and children. Luís likes him a lot and is happy we're going to marry. Sometimes Francisco brings my Mamá and me a box of chocolates, and sometimes beef for grilling, and once even a pink carnation plant in a ceramic bowl.

We plan that I will continue working until I get pregnant, which we hope won't happen for the first year or two. Francisco doesn't mind that they're going to tease him like they tease all the men whose wives don't get pregnant within a few months after marriage—asking them if they don't function, or what? We want to buy our own lot in one of the newer *colonias*, but one that already has electricity, to have something of our own before we start a family. If we pool our savings, we'll be able to get a plot of land in the new *colonia* up the highway in a year or so. If the prices don't go up too much. It's become too expensive to buy one in Colonia Popular, or even in La Unión, where Francisco's parents live, now that both *colonias* have not only electricity, but running water and a sewage system. Then we'll build our house; little by little, like my

brothers are doing, and like my Mamá did here in Colonia Popular.
Estela is going to let me know when they have an opening in the
automobile accessories plant. Then my eyes won't blur so much. If I keep
working at the electronics *maquiladora*, I'll need glasses like my Mamá.

Maybe someday Francisco will let me go back to secretarial school. It
costs a lot for tuition, though. We're going to be living with my Mamá
at first since there is more room in our house than in his. He has seven
brothers and sisters still at home. Three of his brothers are working, so
his Mamá doesn't need him as much as my Mamá does.

My eldest sister is still working on my wedding dress. It will only be a
few weeks more before I stand in the Church and say, "I, María Arenas,
take Francisco Murillo Contreras to be my lawful wedded husband . . ."
And just maybe, we'll be happy, as happy as I am when he takes me by
the hand and leads me out to dance. As happy as I am when he kisses
me goodnight on the edge of my Mamá's lot, before he goes back to his
colonia. Maybe my destiny will be a good one.

Mexicali maquiladora (photo by Fred Lonidier)

Part 2:

Men
In
Colonia Popular

The original version was first published in
Struggle Vol. 9, No. 4, Winter 1993-94, pp. 15-29.

*— I knew Martín's family very well during my first
two years in Colonia Popular. I accompanied the family,
including Martín, his mother Teresa, his stepfather
José and sometimes his sisters to the dump many times,
and worked alongside them collecting cardboard and
other items of interest. I often ate dinner at their house,
providing groceries which Teresa, one of her daughters
or I turned into the evening meal (and saw Martín
dancing with the photographs of his "novias" to amuse
the family). I was co-present with his mother, Teresa,
at many political rallies and social gatherings and co-
present with Martín both on the dump and at numerous
colonia dances.*

The Cartonero (The Cardboard Collector)

I

Martín´s mother woke him an hour before dawn. He scratched the mosquito bites on his face and limbs and feet, picked up the faded red t-shirt lying on the end of the narrow cot, used it to wipe the sweat from his forehead and from under his arms. His mother was already dressed. She had slept in her clothes, too. She handed him his coffee in the large chipped grey mug that had brought home yesterday. "*Buenos días, hijo*" ("Good day, son.) "Your father says we should go in about twenty minutes."

He nodded his assent and thanks, still too sleepy to speak. His stepfather, José, the only father he had ever known, sat on the edge of the large bed, mattress and frame suspended over concrete blocks, across the long rectangular room. His two sisters were still asleep on the other cot, catty-cornered to his own, as were his little brother and youngest sister, who shared a couple of blankets stretched out on the new cement floor.

Martín drank his black sugared coffee fast and went outside to the *palacio*, the palace as his mother called it, the name of the residence of the President of Mexico, to look for a pair of socks. He had to bend to enter the doorway of the small structure formed of irregular battered planks and slivers of planks, the uneven spaces between them filled in by squares and rectangles of plastic cloth and sections of cardboard. The *palacio* had been the family's only shelter when they first arrived from the D.F., the Federal District, and for some years afterwards.

They had a new house for little ore than a year, a large windowless room constructed of even palomino colored planks, with no gaps between the floor and the roof. The Church, with its new interest in the poor, had given his mother the wallboards. Padre Patricio drove them over one day in his new turquoise pick-up, and Martín and his mother and father and friends had nailed them together, fabricating one wall at a time. Then they put up the four sides, nailing them to the four corner posts set deep in cement, leaving an opening for an entrance to be covered with a door they had retrieved from the dump some time ago.

This year the priest had given his mother two hundred thousand pesos, more than the family working together earned in two weeks. Martín was unsure how to feel about this gift. His uncertainty troubled him. Should he feel badly because the churchgoers, in the multi-roomed church filled with blue-robed statues of saints and a seven-foot *Virgén de Guadalupe*, knew that they had less money than anyone among the parishioners? Or content because his mother, who went to every church meeting, retreat, and all the important masses, always available to help serve the refreshments and clean up afterwards, had been selected to receive the special collection given away every year? Or proud because his mother knew how to make money wherever she went, even if it was only a little, even if it was from collecting aluminum cans thrown from car windows when she walked along the highway to visit friends in Colonia Santos?

His mother had spent the two hundred thousand pesos on sacks of cement, and last week Martín had gotten his friends Jorge and Chuco to help mix the contents with coarse sand and water carried from the nearby green canal, using short handled shovels each had brought, in a wheelbarrow they borrowed from the man next door. And they had laid down the new floor. At first they fumbled with the trowels—all except Chuco who had done this work before—then became better at it as the work went on. Now if someone dropped something in the house, if a towel fell to the floor, it didn't come up all dusty. It was harder to sleep on, though, his little brother Adrian had complained.

Martín found a pair of socks among the clumps of clothing piled on the upraised pallet, sat on the edge to pull them on, stepped into his shoes, then, bending, exited to the lot and went over to the bundles of irregularly cut plastic ribbon, discarded from a tarpaulin factory, that they had collected the day before. He grabbed an end of orange plastic material in one hand and stretched the irregularly trimmed lengths across his body, arm-lengths away, doing this three times, then cutting off the measured piece with a rusty pocket knife. He cut about twenty of these three-meter lengths of ribbon, working rapidly, then stopped. Today they would get no more than twenty *pacas* of *carton*, the cardboard they gleaned from the dump to keep on living. They could hope to get between 600 and 800 kilos.

The dump was open in Mexicali, one of the few open dumps in the Republic of Mexico, his *padrastro*, José, had told him. That meant you didn't have to belong to a *síndicato*, or pay off anyone to work in it. His mother would have preferred to live in Ensenada, where it never got so hot or so cold as it did in Mexicali, but where new *colonias* were being settled all the time too. But the dump wasn't open there.

Before they came to live in Mexicali, Martín had helped José and his mother in their job on the municipal dump trucks in the D.F. They went around the city collecting garbage from private houses to take to the dump. Martín's stepfather was a driver's helper on a truck owned by the city and got a salary from the government. José could only be a helper. He couldn't get a driver's license because he couldn't read or write. Not even to sign his name. And buying one cost too much. Even then, he'd have to sign his name. Now he drove their pick-up to the dump without a license.

When they worked for the D.F. garbage collection they would take the *cartón* and metals and put them aside to sell later. Martín's mother also collected clothes for herself and the family, including his sisters and little Adrian. But they couldn't work in any of the capital city's dumps.

In all three dumps you had to pay a percentage of what you collected to the man who had the rights to the garbage. And you had to sell the metal and cardboard you collected to him, too. *Pinche caciques*, José called them. Damned bossmen. And you had to pay a sum to belong to the *síndicato*, so as to get permission to enter the dump and pick over the heaps of refuse. His *padrasto* refused to do this. Garbage should be free, he said.

And it was free in Mexicali. That's one of the reasons they had moved there.

There were some good things about working in the dump. Martín reflected, as he started loading the pick-up, painted in various shades of green, first with a five-gallon bottle of drinking water, then the pile of cut ribbon. He never wanted for clothing, for one thing. He found some every day. Sometimes shoes as well, although it was hard to find a pair together since the bulldozers that leveled the garbage would scatter them. Also the gloves they used while working. His mother had a plastic bag filled with gloves in the yard. And a bag filled with partially used skeins of yarn. And a bag filled with sheets. And a bag of covers. Even an old sleeping bag. The burned-out refrigerator they used to keep the pots and pans and dishes had been found in the dump as well. And the mattresses for the two beds they had build from scrap lumber. Almost everything in the house except the religious pictures of the Last Supper and the Virgin of Guadalupe and the wooden cross with the metal Jesús hanging on it, had come from the dump. Even the posters of flowers and stuffed animals his sister Paula had found and hung up in one corner of the room.

And they could even eat from the dump, for another thing. Sometimes Martín, or his mother Teresa, or his *padrastro* José found canned foods, the containers slightly bent or the labels removed so they had to play a guessing game about what was inside before opening them for dinner. After bringing the canned goods home, they would look carefully at the ends, press them, to see if they were bulging, even slightly.

Because bulging ends meant what someone had called botulism. It could kill you, José had told him.

Sometimes, too, the fish stores dumped the heads of fish they had filleted. The drivers of the trucks bringing the fish heads to the dump would call to the *domperos*, the garbage pickers, to come and get them, before they got soiled from hitting the ground and the garbage stink. The garbage pickers would surround the truck and stick handfuls of fish heads, still attached to their glistening naked spines, into the plastic bags from grocery stores they found in the refuse, turned inside out so the dirty side, which had been filled with garbage, was now outside.

That was one of Martín's favorite meals—fish-head soup. Another one of his favorite meals was *chilaquiles*, hardened tortillas that were fried and covered with a red chili sauce. His mother made that more often because they ate tortillas every day, and there were always some old ones around the house. Sometimes they found boxes filled with them, still in their packages, slightly stiff from age, providing another meal from the dump.

II

Only he, his *padrastro* and his mother were going to the dump today. Martín's 17-year-old sister Ofelia, two years younger than he, had started high school last year, and his 15-year-old sister Paula was finishing junior high. They would be up about 6 to get ready to go.

Martín almost finished secondary school when they lived in the D.F., but he dropped out in ninth grade to work in a factory making notebooks and other school supplies, to help out the family. While he was still in primary school he earned some money sweeping out city buses. He even learned three Vicente Fernández songs and three Lola Beltrán songs and sometimes he would get on a bus and sing, then pass around an old blue baseball cap with "Raiders" printed on it in English, for tips. Last week one of his honeys, a girl whom he danced with at the parties in Fraccionamiento La Nueva occasionally, had given him a Vicente tape. He didn't have a cassette player to listen to it on, though. Maybe he could borrow one from Chuco's sister. Her *madrina* had given her one for her birthday, Martín had heard from Chuco.

Martín knew that his mother though schooling was especially important for his sisters. So they could walk out if they married a worthless *cabrón*, she had said. He had heard her talking about his father. "He preferred dancing to working. And he always found a dancing partner," she recounted. "And he seldom brought money home. Not

even for beans and tortillas." Sometimes Martín felt guilty that his
father had treated his mother that way, as though it were his fault. On
the other hand, he liked to think he was like his father in some ways,
that unknown male responsible for his birth. He always found dancing
partners, too, at every dance. Sometimes four or five. He wondered
sometimes what his father looked like. How he talked. How he danced.

He remembered his mother telling them how she had fed Martín's
two eldest brothers, now married and still living in the D.F., by washing
and ironing clothes for women in the *colonia* bordering theirs on the
outskirts of Mexico City. When she found she was pregnant with him
she left his father, and did the same work until after he was born and
she started living with José. José was a friend on one of her uncles, from
the workshop where they made shoes together for several years after
José arrived in the capital from his *rancho* in Jalisco, in search of work.
Martín's mother had a faded black and white but mostly grey photograph
of them sitting at a workbench nailing leather together, with another
man who had worked there too. Only four men had worked in the shop,
one of them the owner, and he took the photograph according to José,
who, when he had a couple of beers, liked to recall those days and how
he had met and won Martín's mother.

Martín had heard his mother tell his sisters that if they had enough
schooling, even if one of them married a *cabrón* bastard who drank too
much, or hit her, or ran after women, or was a *huevón* too lazy to work,
she could *mandarlo a la chingada*, tell him to go screw himself, and find a
good job to support herself and her children.

Ofelia and Paula still came to the dump when the family worked
in the evenings or on weekends. And in another week school vacations
would begin, so his sisters would accompany them the four or five days
they went each week. Only his thirteen-year old sister Chuey and his
nine-year-old brother Adrian were no longer brought to work in the
dump. Hopefully they were reading ahead in their school lessons when
they were left at home. Probably they were watching the small black-and-
white television his mother had won at a church raffle.

In any case his mother did not want them to come. If they weren't
seen working in the garbage the kids at school could not tease them
about being *domperos*, as they had Ofelia until she got in a fight and came
home too early from the school one day.

Martín remembered only too well the afternoon she had arrived,
tears streaming down her cheeks, refusing to talk at first. Finally, she told
him and their mother that some kid had started in on her, when they
were choosing sides for a volleyball game during the lunch break, saying

that she was just a *dompera*, and asking who would want a *dompera*, a garbage vulture, on their side?

Martín had walked out of the house, feeling helpless, shaking inside. That night he got in his first fist fight in Mexicali, with a couple of boys from La Nueva. Chuco was constantly asking him to come to that better-off *colonia* to get some joker who was always making remarks about the *piojos* (fleas) who lived in Colonia Popular. That evening Martín went. He hoped it was the same guy who had bothered his sister. In any case he and Chuco beat the crap out of the joker and his *cuate*, neither of whom had even done a day of hard labor in their lives. His mother found out about it a couple of days later. "Don't ever do that again. For any reason," she told him. "Those *hijos de sus madres* will go and complain and you'll land in jail. Then how do you think I am going to find money to get you out?"

That night too, he met as usual with his *cuates* from the *colonia*, who gathered outside Doña Angela's soda pop and candy store to drink sodas and sometimes beer and rap and eye the girls as they passed on their way to Doña Petra's *tienda* to buy tortillas or on some other errand. But this time, and from now on, he was among those who whistled loudest, and competed most strenuously to think up outrageous comments to hurl at the feminine presences. "*Mi vida*, when are you coming to dance with me?" "Do you want me to accompany you so no one else gets you first?" "Don't be afraid, I'm only as dangerous as you think I am." "One little kiss will do." The girls would sometimes giggle, behind a modest hand raised to cover mouth, but never answer. As good girls they just hurried along their way. But some seemed to find errands to do almost every night Martín was on the corner with they boys.

He often told his *cuates* about his adventures, the things he had seen. About dances in the D.F. and around Mexicali in the *colonias* where they had not been, about the time Super Barrio had come to visit Ciudad Netza while he was living there, about the time his boss in the school supplies factory had taken him and some others to Acapulco where they drank beer on the beach for three days when he was only fifteen, and saw honeys from all over in bikinis, and about the time he went with his friend Jorge, now married so no longer hanging out with them as much, to Ensenada, where they stayed in Jorge's uncle's house, and "*Cabrón* does he have pretty cousins!"

But now he began telling them about all his honeys, pulling forth photographs guarded in his shirt pocket, showing them the pictures of wavy-haired girls dressed in low-cut evening gowns and matching earrings and necklaces, pictures he had found in the dump, discarded from photographic studios whose names were stamped on the back. He picked one of the photographs and told, to the admiring, half-believing gazes, how he had danced with her at the Plaza Cachanilla when Los Bukis played there two months ago, and how he was thinking of bringing her to the La Nueva dance competition next week, but maybe not because she'd cling to him too much and he wanted to *cumbia* with Jorge's sister-in-law who had just come from Sinaloa to live in the *colonia* and looked at him a lot when she came to buy tortillas a couple of days ago when he was standing outside of Doña Petra's store.

Martín had often entertained his mother and sisters with his imaginary honeys too, making the whole family laugh as he danced around the room holding himself and blowing noisy kisses at the photographs and weaving magical stories about the girls and where he had met them and where he had taken them and where they had invited him. Sometimes, too, he told his mother about his real honeys, those who had flung him a glance or cast him a smile or with whom he had danced, embracing them closely, to Los Caminantes or Los Tigres del Norte cassettes played at the *colonia quinceañera* and birthday parties and weddings. She would smile with pleasure in her light brown eyes, and say, "My handsome son," and tell him he was young and should have all the sweethearts he wanted—until he married.

She didn't want him to marry, he knew. Sometimes she asked, "What could you want that you don't have here. Ofelia and me to cook for you. Chuey to wash for you." Paula didn't like to do household chores, so she was seldom mentioned, but she was most like him, loving to dance, spinning around the room with him, matching him step for step, when La Sonora Dinamita or Los Yonics appeared on a television program.

He always answered, bending down to kiss her on the forehead. "Nothing Mamá. And I have the most beautiful Mamá in the world. My *padrastro* is jealous every time you leave the house alone." A wife would be another mouth to feed. Neither Martín nor his mother wanted a wife of his to work in the dump. Even if she did, soon more demanding, little mouths would come along. He still had time for these things. Better lots of honeys anyway.

With lots of honeys he'd have more stories to tell his *cautes*, too.

But Martín wanted to take revenge on the boy who had teased his sister about being a *dompera*. He got Chuco's sister, who was in school with Ofelia, to find out who he was. He knew Ofelia would not tell him, fearing he would get in a fight. Chuco's sister did find out though. Then, at La Nueva dances, Martín started watching him, this guy named Efren, noted who he was talking to, what girls he was looking at, who he was dancing with, until he found out which girl was Efren's favorite.

One *quinceañera* party several months later, Martín made his move. He began by asking some of the prettier girls to dance, those he had danced with before, so he knew they would not refuse him. He danced smoothing, effortlessly, as he had learned to dance since the age of fourteen, moving the way he did the two times he had won the dance contests in the D.F. He danced as though he were on camera, making sure Efren's favorite noticed him, showing his partners moves they had never seen before, making they look better than they'd even look with anyone else.

After the break he went over to the bright-eyed shapely girl Efren was always looking at, usually dancing with when he danced, and politely asked her for the next *ranchera*. Just as politely, she refused. Martín seldom insisted, he felt it discourteous, just walked way with a "Gracías. Maybe next time," if a chosen partner said no. But this time he said, "You have a *novio* or something? You're afraid he'll be jealous?"

She replied, looking him straight in the eyes, not smiling, "I don't dance with just anyone." Martín turned away, disappointed.

The same night there was a dance contest. Martín asked Chuco's little sister to be his partner, since they had danced a lot together and she could follow him easily. He didn't dance as well as usual, though, so they just came in third. His only satisfaction was that Efren and his honey, the girl who refused to dance with "just anyone" didn't even make it into the last five considered.

III

His mother came out of the house, went over to the bag of gloves and grabbed a handful of them, counting out a pair for herself, for José, for Martín. Martín jumped into the back of the pick-up. He bound a folded red bandana around his forehead, tying it in the back, to keep his light brown hair, inherited from his French great grandfather his mother had told him, out of his eyes while he was working.

His *padrastro* and mother got into the cab of the truck, his mother struggling with the door that seldom opened without much pulling and jerking. She finally got the door open and climbed inside, slamming it shut hard so it would not fly open when they bounced over the rutted roads. José backed the pick-up down the small hill, out of the lot, turned right, then left at the corner and headed the few hundred meters toward the dump; the tires brought up small puffs of pulverized clay that expanded and merged to cloud the streets in their wake.

The dump was almost empty of people when they arrived. Only two boys were working, with *ganchos*, raking the wet remains of fruit and vegetables and opened food containers away to hook open the plastic bags below in the hopes of finding aluminum cans.

Martín yelled over to them, "*Qué vole?* What's up?" The tallest raised his hand, shouted a greeting back. Martín knew almost everyone on the dump, but one of the boys was new.

He walked over and gave Chon the special handshake the *cuates* from the *colonias* knew, then turned to the other *muchacho*. "You from here?"

"Now I am. I'm Ramón." They shook hands, though Ramón did not know the whole symbol system yet.

"Where are you from?" Martín asked.

"Tijuana."

"Ever work in a dump before?"

"We used to *live* in the dump. In Tijuana," Ramón replied.

Martín hesitated for a moment. His family had never had it that bad. They'd always have some place to go home to. He searched for some commonality. "We used to stay weekends on the dump. When we first came to Mexicali. It was over at the airport then. My . . . ." He hesitated again, as always never knowing what to call José, not liking to broadcast it that his mother had been married before, "father wanted to save gas."

"Where'd you sleep, in the truck?" Ramón asked.

"My mother did. And José. That's my . . . . my father's name. And my sisters. I used to collect some *cartón* and spread it out and me and my brother Adrian slept on that. You have mosquitoes in Tijuana?"

"No. At least not like here. You can't get away from them. *Hijos de sus chingadas madres.*"

Martín laughed. "*Pinches sangudos,*he agreed. "Get some lace curtains while you're collecting. They work like a mosquito net. I'm looking for some for my bed too."

He left them then, to rejoin his mother and José.

José had found an old boat motor, taken over to where the truck was parked. He would probably be able to find some working parts to yank out that some junkyard owner would want to buy if he couldn't get it to work and sell the whole thing.

Teresa began flattening the pieces of *cartón* she and José had accumulated, tearing the few rectangular boxes down their corners and folding the sides in on the base. Martín selected a piece of plastic ribbon and went over to help her. He tied a small loop in one end, then stretched out the three meter length. He gathered the cardboard his mother had flattened, setting it in the middle of the outstretched ribbon, piece on top of piece, unless the pieces were small, then two pieces beside one another. He helped her break up the rest of the boxes and added them to the pile. When the *paca* was big enough, somewhere between 30 and 40 kilos, Martín bound it, first crosswise, pulling the end of the plastic ribbon through the loop, then lengthwise, like a Christmas package, tying the loose end in the middle, near the top.

He heaved the bulk up onto his back. He weighed only 20 or 30 kilos more than it did. He trotted it over, slightly off balance, to where the truck was parked, starting a pile of *pacas* beside it. Then he went back to help his mother with the second pack.

By 6:30 they still had only three *pacas*. But work would pick up later on. José had found some meters of electrical cord, which he stripped to cut out the copper wire. Usually he didn't do this until they got home, but the garbage trucks hadn't begun coming.

A little before 7:00 more *domperos* arrived. There were now eighteen. Martín counted them, as they worked through the garbage with their hooks, leisurely, waiting for the first garbage trucks to arrive. A friend of his, also a *cartonero*, specialized in collecting cardboard, came walking across the dump toward him. They rapped awhile: "How're you doing? Where's you're little brother?"

"He's coming along with the bicycle in a bit," Maxi replied. Maxi and Javier didn't have a pick-up truck only a bicycle built from parts of other bicycles scavenged from the garbage. That meant they had to sell to the buyers who came to the dump. They earned 10 thousand pesos a ton from selling to these buyers.

It was good Maxi's brother was coming. A couple of weeks ago he had slipped and fallen and cut his leg on a piece of broken glass when he was pulling cardboard from under a pile of other garbage. It was a deep cut and he couldn't work for some days and was still limping the last time Martín had seen him. Their widowed mother was dependent on their income from the dump, and there was less income with only one working.

And it was hard for a *cartonero* to work alone because one person has to grab the cardboard from the mound of garbage if it was dumped from the municipal dump trucks or off the back of a pick-up, throwing it behind him, depending on a partner to keep it in a separate pile. When there were a lot of *cartoneros* everyone threw their cardboard behind them and if there was no partner to keep it separated no one knew which cardboard belonged to which *cartonero*. Usually they just separated it into equal piles without much fuss. Sometimes, though, people wanted to claim more cardboard than they had grabbed. Martín didn't mind just dividing it evenly, in the case of a dispute, though he often lost out by doing so. Young and strong, he managed to grab more cardboard than the women *cartoneras* or the older male *cartoneros*.

The first municipal garbage truck appeared at the entrance to the dump. Martín ran toward the northern edge of the dump, where the truck was headed, as did the other *domperos*. The truck disgorged its contents into a large pile. The garbage-pickers swarmed around the mound, some climbing on top of it, working with their hooks, pulling plastic bags filled with garbage toward themselves, tearing them open, grabbing the cans or clothing or shoes or anything else of interest from the, then threw these things into their collection bags. One *dompero* threw a pile of newspapers he found to the bent, white-haired woman who specialized in newsprint resale. She nodded her thanks, gathered them up.

Martín and Maxi began grabbing cardboard boxes, emptying their contents, if any, on the garbage mound, throwing them back behind them. Teresa looked quickly through the clothing, picked up a couple of pieces, inspected them to see if they were ripped or stained or misshapen, discarded most of them, put a sweater for Chuey into her bag. Then, reaching for some lengths of cardboard, she carried them to where Martín was throwing cardboard boxes behind him. She pulled these to one side, and began breaking the boxes into flat pieces. José came with a length of ribbon, stretched it out, then moved to help Martín, pulling square and rectangular pieces of cardboard from the truckload-full pile of garbage. Martín grabbed for a large piece of flattened cardboard sticking out from under the mound, pulled it out from under the weight of the *basura*, threw it beside the pile his mother was making on top of the orange binder ribbon.

Another dump truck arrived. Martín and some of the other *domperos* moved toward this truck, others stayed behind on the first mound, still picking through the garbage. Martín's stepfather came to help him, both throwing the cardboard boxes and pieces of cardboard into a pile. Teresa finished breaking up the cardboard for the pack beside the first hill of garbage, and moved to separate and break up the cardboard being thrown off the second mound by her husband and her son. Soon José turned to help her in this task, and Martín ran to bind up the pile of cardboard at the first disgorgement to get it out of the way of the oncoming bulldozer. He bound it, picked it up, trotted it over to the truck. He grabbed some more lengths of ribbon from the back of the pick-up, sticking some in his pants pocket, getting another ready to bind up the packs his mother and José were working on. More *cartoneros* had arrived.

Martín began to tie up one of the *pacas*, then, sighting two private pick-ups entering the dump, left this task to José. He had noted one was filled with cardboard, and the other trash. He whistled to get Maxi's attention. "*Vamónos*, let's go," he yelled, motioning toward the pick-up.

Martín and Maxi ran, reached the moving pick-up, leapt up on it, began separating the cardboard from the rest of the garbage, Maxi to one side, Martín to the other. When the driver stopped, Martín and Maxi began throwing cardboard off, each to his own side. Maxi's brother arrived and began putting Maxi's into a pile. Teresa came over to help Martín. José joined her after carrying the last bound pack over to their growing pile of packs. Martín found a cardboard box filled with a couple of heads of lettuce with wilted outer leaves, a few tomatoes with one or two rotten spots, and a number of dry-skinned oranges. He whistled to his mother, handed her the box.

Martín turned to the driver: "Want me to clean it for you?" The driver, a close-shaven forty, well-dressed in a white shirt and cowboy boots, nodded his assent. Martín reached for the broom leaning against the back of the cab and began pushing off the garbage, mostly cut grass and tree branches, out of the back of the turquoise pick-up. This done, he swept the pick-up clean. The driver handed him a two thousand peso bill, as Martín leapt off. He had known he would earn something. And this was his to keep, to pay for his sodas.

His mother was eating one of the oranges. Martín bent for one, began to peel it. Ate it quickly. Then he picked up the box containing the oranges and took it over beside José's pick-up truck, leaving José and his mother to break down and bind the cardboard. As he walked back in their direction he tied a loop in another length of ribbon. At least two more *pacas* had come off the turquoise pick-up. He started running toward them, seeing the bulldozer headed their way. They would have to get the cardboard over to one side before tying it up. The three carried the cardboard away from the bulldozer's route, lost a few smaller pieces.

Garbage trucks were arriving every five or ten minutes now. Martín concentrated on running to the mounds, hauling cardboard from them, breaking it up into flattened pieces, piling them up, binding the cardboard into a *paca*, carrying it over to José's pick-up. His mother and stepfather sometimes helped him, sometimes worked together, apart. He and José did most of the gathering, and all of the carrying. But his mother did everything except carry the packs. She was too little, scarcely five feet tall, and only weighed about as much as one of the bigger *pacas* anyway. One woman *cartonera* did carry, but the friend she worked with would set the pack on her back. Almost only men could lift the weight into place alone.

By 9 a.m. more than a hundred *domperos* were working. It was summer now, so by noon most would leave, to take a break while the temperatures reached 120 degrees Farenheit. Some would return again after 4 p.m.

It was when Martín was pulling cardboard out of the newest heap of garbage left by a factory cleanup truck that the bulldozer driven by Don Ernesto, flattening down and pushing refuse outwards, forming the ever-expanding plateau, propelling hundreds of kilos of it over into the arroyo, came his way. Martín knew to keep the cardboard out of the way of the two bulldozers, but especially the one with Don Ernesto at the controls. Don Ernesto drove as though there were no *domperos*. He ran right over the piles of cardboard and plastic bags of stuff the garbage-pickers had collected, began to bulldoze as soon as the garbage was deposited, did not give the pickers even a minute or two to shift through the mound as the other driver did. Teresa had heard him say that he didn't care if he hit one of the *domperos* since no one could fine him for doing his job and the *domperos* had no legal right to be in the dump anyway.

Martín leapt out of the way of the bulldozer just in time. But then he noticed Doña Ramona's youngest daughter, trying to pull a doll, one arm missing, out of a plastic bag of garbage, right in the way of the oncoming bulldozer, but too close for Don Ernesto to see her. As she looked up, the hill of garbage, propelled resolutely forward, began moving around her, the lighter pieces flung up into the air, then falling, to be picked up again. She started to move away, still holding on to the one good arm of the amputated doll, but the mound of garbage had trapped one of her legs. She was going to be pushed under, buried beneath the refuse.

Martín moved rapidly toward her, putting up one hand, yelling, "Stop!" to Don Ernesto, who didn't hear him over the roaring of the motor, the clang and trashing of metal and trash. Martín got to her, grabbed her under both arms, pulled her out from the muck now up around her waist. Don Ernesto slowed for a split second upon seeing Martín run in front of him, then continued on, pushing the garbage out and down, tens of meters downward into the gaping arroyo.

As Martín jumped to one side, he slipped, went down on one knee, kept slipping, over broken glass, ripping away at his pant leg, gashing into his shin. Doña Ramona and Martín's mother and Maxi arrived about the same time. Doña Ramona embraced her daughter, then shook her, repeating, "You've got to be careful." As the blood ran down his leg, Martín's mother grabbed a t-shirt protruding from a small heap of garbage and told Maxi: "Bring me a head of lettuce from the box. Over by the pick-up. Quick!"

When she got the head of lettuce she tore off the wilted outer leaves, then handed Martín a few of the inner leaves, told him to put them over his cuts. Martín took the t-shirt from her and bound the lettuce, the only sanitary covering available, in place. "It's not real deep, ma," he said. "It's not half as bad as Javier's was."

Don Ernesto stopped for a moment as he was backing up to begin a new run, shook his head. "You all have got to watch your kids. I'm not a *pinche* babysitter," he said, for anyone who wanted to hear.

"*Chinga tu madre*," said Maxi, under his breath. Martín smiled, gave Maxi a thumbs-up in agreement.

"Let me buy you a soda," Doña Ramona said after ascertaining that the wound was not deep. But Martín refused. "No. That's O.K. You don't owe me anything. We all got to look out for each other here." Doña Ramona smiled, patted him on his shoulder, and returned to collecting the clothing she washed and ironed and sold from door-to-door in the poorer *colonias*. Her daughter, having finally extricated the doll from the plastic bag that she had clasped throughout her adventure, stayed close by her side.

As Martín and his mother walked over toward the side of the dump where the pick-ups were parked, Martín limping slightly, he said, "She doesn't even have enough to buy sodas for her kids." Teresa replied, "Well, let's get one anyway."

They went over to the mobile cart owned by the widow who sold sodas for 500 pesos apiece, along with *tortas*, to the garbage pickers, coming each day to do so. As they stood drinking their bottles of Coca Cola, Teresa looked up at Martín. "You're a good kid," she smiled. She paused, then touched him lightly on the jaw with her first. "What kid? You're not a kid anymore. You're a man. Worth any two *cabrones*."

They returned to work, Martín insisting he was all right. That she should have seen Maxi's brother Javier when he cut himself if she wanted to see blood.

By 11 a.m. they had seventeen *pacas*.

IV

The *cuates* from the *colonia* had heard about him saving the little girl. They slapped him on the back, punched him in the arm, asked him to show them his cuts, got him to tell them what happened. He told them of the villainous Don Ernesto, the dangers of working in the dump, for the benefit of those who did not already know, and to the nods of those who already did. Those who did added their own stories. Jorge, Ramona's first cousin, bought him a liter of Tecate.

He felt good.

V

That Saturday night he won the dance competition in La Nueva, injured leg and all. He even beat the *cholo* who came in from Tijuana with Doña Florinda's famous daughter. Both of them dressed in expensive black rags, the guy in tight pegged pants and pointed shoes and a leather jacket with zippers everywhere and the honey in a bitty little skirt, showing off her round little tail like she did at the dance halls in T.J., with a French beret tilted to one side of her head and long silver-colored earrings bouncing back and forth. He had won almost single-handed, since his partner for the dance competition, though one of the prettiest honeys in La Nueva, just sort of paced in place while he jived and shook and shimmied around her, copying some of the moves of Emmanuel, the singer who his mother said he resembled. Few could outdance him. He might be a *dompero* but he was *bien chingón*.

Efren and his honey did not place.

After the competition the honey he had won with introduced him to her cousin, who lived in Pueblo Nuevo on the other side of Mexicali, but had come over to visit his relatives in La Nueva. Partially to keep an eye on his cousin Julia, whose *novio*, a friend of his, lived in the same *colonia* he did. The *novio* was in San Bernadino for the next few weeks, though.

Martín found out from Julia's cousin that they were hiring packers at the Coca Cola plant on Justo Sierra. "Why don't you come over and fill out a form? You've finished primary, haven't you?"

Martín replied that he had almost finished secondary, asked how much the company paid.

"One hundred and twenty thou a week," the cousin answered. "But after three months you get *seguro*, so you and your family can get free medical care."

Martín figured that it was more than his work in the dump was paying. With the whole family working they earned more than any two could earn at factory work. But his *padrastro*, José, was getting old. He was either 53 or 54. No one knew for sure because his birth had never been registered and his mother had died when he was 10 or 11, back on the *rancho* in Jalisco where he was from.

Martín knew that José would like to become a buyer in the dump now that it was getting hard for him to lift and haul the *pacas*. But there was never enough money in the house to exchange for all the cardboard even one *cartonero* collected in a week. And if they couldn't pay for the cardboard when it was offered, the *cartoneros* would look for someone else to sell to, someone who they were sure could buy all the cardboard they had packed in whenever they had it on hand.

Maybe if he went to work in the factory they could use some of the cash for buying, Martín thought.

He looked at the cousin. "Got many honeys working there?"

"More than half the plant is *puras muchachas. Bien bonitas.* Pretty ones," the cousin answered, taking a swig of beer, then offering the bottle to Martín.

"Maybe I'll try it out," said Martín, thinking of all the stories he could tell his *cuates*. And his Mamá and sisters. And his Papá.

Garbage pickers, Mexicali, 1993 (photo by author)

Working on the Dump, 1993" (photo by author)

A cardboard collector, Mexicali dump, 1993 (photo by author)

The original version was published in *Struggle*, Vol. 10, No. 1, Spring 1994, pp. 12-20.

— I knew Jesús´s employer and co-workers and often went with sisters and wives—who sometimes brought them their noonday meals—to the Plaza Cachanilla when it was under construction. I lunched there with his family shortly after the Plaza was opened—and a few times more over the ensuing years—and went there with him and his friends just to wander and look around several times after it was completed.

The Tablaroquero (The Drywaller)

I

The day had finally come. Jesús was going to take his father and
mother, two sisters and two brothers to lunch at the Plaza Cachanilla,
where he had worked as a drywaller, finishing the interior of a luxurious
department store. Over two months time he had saved up a week's salary,
150 thousand pesos, more than most people in his *colonia* earned, more
than anyone else in his family earned. He had given his mother the
usual 100 thousand a week for family expenses, tried to spend no more
than 20 thousand a week for the several sodas he needed each day to get
him through the sweltering temperatures sweating away all the liquid
he consumed as he carried the heavy, door-shaped slabs of drywalling,
riveting them into place. And each week he put aside 20 to 30 thousand
pesos, just so he could take them there, invite them there for lunch.

It had meant he'd had to go without drinking beer with his *cuates*
at the Saturday night dances in La Nueva, not accepting more than a
sip when a bottle was passed around, not accepting a whole bottle even
when it was offered him, because when it came his turn he could not buy
a round. It also meant he was still wearing his old work boots with the
heel that kept flapping loose on the left one, no matter how much glue
he used on it.

But he wanted his family to see the Plaza, a place unlike any other
they'd ever seen before. From the time he was born until they invaded
a lot in Colonia Popular eight years ago, they had lived on brickyards
or in empty spaces behind gas stations or along some highway without
lights or running water, as they had for the first four years after getting
their lot in the *colonia*, until, after many demonstrations and petitionings
at governmental offices led by *la presidente*, Doña Socorro, electricity
was extended to the *colonia* residents. They had never gone anywhere so
beautiful, colorful, luxurious.

The family got into the rusting Ford Pinto station wagon with its
crumbled front fender. Fernando, his next youngest brother, who loved
to drive, and who was the only one besides his father who had saved up
enough to get a driver's license, crawled in behind the wheel. The others
climbed into the back seat, his youngest brother Pablo continuing on
to the luggage carrier, finding a space beside the battery jumper cables,
the patched spare tire, and a variety of tools. He himself sat in the front
bucket seat beside Fernando because the transmission was getting erratic

and whenever they had to go in reverse someone had to get out and push. Pablo, who enjoyed playing with car motors, was going to try to fix it someday, whenever they had enough money to go to the junkyard and find parts.

They drove down the stretch of dirt road then turned right on the highway running past the *colonia*. At the Sánchez Toboada crossing they took the rutted Lázaro Cárdenas Boulevard north, past the family selling plums and mangos on one corner, through the dense air filled with the fumes of a thousand exhaust pipes. They had to stop at the red light across from the Sakura restaurant when they were almost half way to the Plaza. Jesús wondered if he'd ever be able to take his family to that restaurant. He had helped finish the interior there, too, but it was really expensive, and he had never heard of anything on the menu anyway. But he liked to imagine his mother in a place like that, with chandeliers and hanging plants and a waterway with a bridge, she who got up at 5 a.m. each morning to make the *burritos* he and Pablo, and Fernando when he was employed, took to work. He had heard advertisements for the Sakura restaurant on the *ranchera* station they listened to on the radio. Many times. It made him proud, but a little sad, too, knowing that no one in his family, no one he even knew, not even the contractor he had worked for putting in the drywall, would ever get to eat there or to see his work.

II

The first thing they came to when they entered the multi-domed mall was a game room with billiards, shuffleboard tables, electronic games, pin-ball machines, and even a section for small children containing a miniature carousel and ponies and camels and elephants that rocked and spun and hopped if you put a thousand peso coin in the slot. Immediately his littlest sister, Rosita, now in third grade, said, "Mamá, can we go in?" His mother looked at him and he nodded. He hadn't been there himself.

Rosita stood a moment before the tiny carousel, built for little children, younger than she now was at almost ten. Jesús watched her as she discovered the small grey-painted elephant with upturned trunk, the pinto pony, the palomino one behind it, followed by a dark blonde camel, all adorned with saddles and bridles in reds and purples, greens and blues, all going up and down and around in smooth synchronic motion. Jesús saw Rosita looking at his mother, smiling, pointing, then his mother and two sisters moved on, Rosarita now too big for such a diminutive version of a circus world, to explore the large room filled with diversions of many mechanical kinds.

He and Pablo and Fernando began walking around as well, stopped to watch some guys their age play pool. "We should come play billiards sometime," Fernando said. "O.K.," replied Jesús, watching a shot. They had played billiards a couple of times downtown in the red light district when their friend Gumi, Luís's brother, had invited them.

Jesús watched his mother, Rosita and Estela go over to the nearby shuffleboard table, heard Rosita murmur something to her mother, heard his mother tell Rosita they didn't have money for games. He hadn't planned on this added expense, but thought it would be a nice memory for them. It was only a thousand pesos a game, about half an American dollar. He took out a five-thousand-peso note, walked over and handed it to his mother, said, "It's for Rosita and Estela to play something." His mother smiled back in thanks. She went to get change and then began playing shuffleboard with Rosita, while his father looked on. Estela went over and a stuck a coin their mother had given her into a game with basketballs bouncing around in a glass cage. Jesús and his brothers went over to the pac-man and race-car driver machines, and there went another six thousand pesos.

His father rounded them all up after his mother and Rosita had played three rounds of shuffleboard and they went out to the arched wing with its gigantic earth-colored flowerpots taller than Rosita and filled with plants.

"They're rather stunted," said his father, fingering a mountain gardenia's green leaf edged in brown. "Not enough light," said his mother. Jesús nervously fingered the yellow-handed screwdriver he always carried in his back pocket, feeling the criticism as though it had been directed at him. But he felt better when his mother admired the large polished stone earns along the second archway that could hold, as she said, even a small *guasave*, or *limón* or *guayaba* tree.

As they neared the center of the Plaza where they were to eat, Rosita and Estela pulled the family into a small department store, toward a table filled with stuffed animals and dolls on sale for 20 and 30 thousand pesos. They all looked though the assorted playthings, picking up a large white bear with a blue ribbon collar and a matching baby bear stuck in a pouch in her stomach, a spotted dog wearing a vest that said "Embrace me," a long-limbed brown money with button eyes, a red-haired clown in a multicolored clown suit and oversized shoes and carrying a small drum.

Rosita, clutching the clown, looked up at their mother and said shyly, "Mamá, can I have one?" Jesús looked at the price. Thirty thousand pesos. He glanced at his father. His father shook his head. Jesús did too.

He only had enough money left for lunch and ice cream afterwards. His father had put all the money he had saved these past few months into buying wood so they could build a kitchen, and sacks of cement so it could have a real floor. The stove was now in the room shared by his parents and sisters, in the original scrap-wood shelter they had erected on the lot, where they all had lived until three years ago. Almost four years ago his father had left the back breaking labor of brickmaking, after he fell from the roof of their house that he had ascended to repair and broken his clavicle. Soon afterwards, he had gotten a job as a night watchman. Jesús and Fernando had stopped making bricks as well, and found waged jobs. With the money he and Fernando had given to his mother, after school expenses were taken out for Rosita and Estela and Pablo, all of whom were still in primary school then, his father had bought second-hand materials for the room the boys built and where the three of them now slept. The family hoped to have three rooms someday, with smooth, even pine planks and with windows with glass panes, a kitchen-sitting room and two bedrooms. Once they were built, the eight-year-old shack, window spaces hung with burlap bags, floor turned to mud when it rained, would be demolished. Jesús, all of them, looked forward to that day, which would mean a new, more comfortable life had replaced the old.

Jesús's mother ruffled her hand though some packaged socks at a nearby table, checked the price. Then they left. Whether in a downtown shoe or clothing store or a temporary *tanguis*, like those that came in trucks to the *colonias*, they were used to looking and not buying. A few seconds later they came to the very center of the Plaza with its large round columns, three feet in diameter, framing the seating area where lavender parasols hovered over the gleaming white tables and their four attached chairs. Rosita, her eyes pierced by colors, gasped, "Mamá. It looks like a carnival. How beautiful." Their mother looked up toward the ceiling made of lightly smoked glass, successive rectangular pieces of opaqueness, each sheltered in a metal frame, suspended over double arches painted pale pink and rose and gray, lined in turquoise. "Yes," she agreed, "it is." Jesús looked down at the toe of his work boot, pleased, as if he had given a present that was well received.

"Look at the fountain," his father said, and pointed to the center of the seating area. They walked over, studied the water falling down through the three carved stone tiers into the gray bottom lined with navy tiles punctuated by rows and occasional diamond shapes of white. His mother bent, ran the water through her hand. Rosita and Estela echoed her gesture. Pancho stood and watched the cascade, his hands in his pockets, unconsciously copying Jesús.

"Let's walk around and see what we'll have for lunch," Jesús said after awhile. Fast-food restaurants lined each elongated side of the central plaza. They began on one side, first passing "*Sarai n' Titos*", which advertised *bistek ranchera* for 14 thousand pesos and *chimichanga* with salad for 10 thousand, past a place which sold miniature hot dogs, two for 5 thousand, then a Chinese take-out, "*La Pequeña Dragón*" with a special for 7,500 pesos. Altogether there were three Chinese stalls, Jesús noticed. He and his family had once been to a fancy wedding in the *colonia* where his cousin Javier lived, and they had served a Chinese dinner. He had especially liked the shrimp with mushrooms, but they didn't seem to offer that here.

At the end was a pizza place. A large pepperoni was 36 thousand pesos. He had eaten pizza once, with ham, when Luís had taken him and the rest of the drywaller crew out for dinner once when they were working in Rosarito.

On the other side of the interior plaza were more food stalls, one selling *tacos de carne asada*, at 2,500 each. They were so small you needed at least six of them to fill up, maybe just four for the girls, Jesús thought. Another place selling hamburgers, another ice cream cones. Two Chinese restaurants and a Japanese one with the same name as the luxurious one he had helped to finish. They offered Yaki Soba for 9 thousand pesos, but he didn't know what Yaki Soba was. They also offered shrimp cocktails for 13 thousand pesos, almost the daily minimum wage.

"Well, Ma, what would you like?" Jesús asked. She shrugged. Smiled. "Let's walk around again," she said.

"Want to try a pizza?" he asked. Rosita answered enthusiastically. "Yes. Yes. I want some pizza." She added, referring to a friend of their mother's whose husband's father owned the small trucking company for which he brother Pablo now worked, "Sandra had pizza at her house once." "It's good," agreed Pablo, "She gave me a piece too." Fernando smiled, shrugged, looking like their mother.

"Here, Ma," Jesús said, handing her a 100 peso bill. "Get two. With pepperoni. And sodas."

"We'll get the tables," Fernando said. The two girls went with their mother, to help her carry back lunch.

They waited until two adjoining tables were vacated. Jesús's mother and sisters arrived soon afterwards with the pizzas and Pepsis.

They ate their slices of pizza, looking around them, Fernando and Jesús eyeing a girl or two. They enjoyed being among the people, the taste of an unusual food, the smell of jasmine growing from the earthed-in sections of the four-tiered false gateways covered with cream-colored and dark rose tiles.

Rosita looked up at the brightly painted arches, she who had never spent time within walls of anything but weathered scrapwood, or at best the smooth unpainted planks of her brothers' bedroom or the new primary school in Colonia Popular.

She asked to anyone who might want to answer, "What do you see that's different from what you've ever seen?"

Estela answered, looking down, "Well, there's a finished floor. And plants all around."

Rosita responded, somewhat impatiently, "So does Sandra's house have a finished floor. And Uncle Estebán's. And so does the social center. And the school. And my Mamí has plants all around our lot."

Estela answers, "But not with tiles on them. Dark gray sprinkled tiles on white like a wild bird's egg." Such expensive tiles they would never have, she knew. Not even the houses of the better off in the *colonia*, like Sandra's, had such flooring.

Rosita pointed upward to the arches. "Look at all the colors." She turns to her mother, "Mamí, when we build our new house can we have all those colors?"

Their mother laughed. "I just want a kitchen someday with yellow walls. The color of canaries. And maybe some canaries too."

Jesús turned to his father, repeated Rosita's question, "What do you think Papa? What do you see here that makes it different from other places?"

Jesús's father looked around him, notices a woman walking by, wearing purple patent high-heeled shoes and a pearl necklace, a man by her side in white shirt, cuffs turned back, and tie, notices the table of teenagers, the girls wearing skirts of the newest style, a young man with a shiny portable cassette player starkly emitting the newest Anna Gabriel song, and then he answers, "All social classes come here."

Fernando jumps in, "From we the millionaires to the *más piojos*, those who are the most lice-bitten."

Their mother laughs, "If we are the millionaires, how is it going with the poor ones?"

As the family took up this theme, Jesús wondered about buying the clown for Rosita. She had never had a brand new toy, just bears with one ear or leg torn off, a plastic doll with face melted from being to close to a stove, a rag doll with patches of hair missing, once a rabbit without his cottontail, discarded items they'd found in the dump, like all of them had had.

The clown could sit on his mother's new cupboard. The one his father had bought from Don José who had brought it back from the relocated dump several weeks ago. His father had painted it sky blue with the paint left over from a week-end job Fernando had taken at La Nueva. They would all enjoy the toy, remember their day at the Plaza.

It would mean not buying ice cream. But maybe next time. He hadn't told them he was going to buy ice cream cones afterwards anyway.

"Let's go get Rosita's clown," Jesús announced. His mother looked startled, but didn't say anything. His father raised his eyebrows and smiled. Rosita smiled, too, looking at her eldest brother lovingly.

After Jesús paid for the clown, Rosita insisted upon carrying it, alternately gazing at the new gift and hugging it to her chest, and Jesús's mother folded up the plastic bag the salesgirl had put the toy into and slipped it into her purse for some later use. Then Jesús led the family down another corridor, to show them the department store he had helped finish, before they drove home.

"Here it is, Ma," Jesús said, as they entered. "Look up there." "Oh Mamí, look," Rosita and Estela said at the same time, pointing up to the mural of a life-sized tiger stalking toward them though a fern-filled jungle, its elongated incisors glistening.

"Luís brought a friend of his all the way up from Mexico City to paint that," Jesús said proudly.

Then Jesús's mother and sisters began to look though the clothing. Jesús saw Estela's face light up with pleasure as she took down a black velvet dress with brocaded sleeves and matching ruffle at the bottom of the smooth full skirt, brocade of dark blue and green and aqua pierced by golden threads on a midnight background, held it up before her. Jesús's mother checked the size, sought the price. Then, with a stunned look, she placed it back on the hanger and back on the rack, and moved away.

Jesús walked over and looked at the tag. Handwritten in red over the original price of 500,000 pesos was the new price of 429,000 pesos. Even on sale it was almost three times his weekly salary.

Jesús felt a sudden anger clamp at his intestines and temples. Teeth clenched, realizing how far from his world these things were, this place was, he glanced up at the tiger, its red mouth open, its fangs showing.

He turned to his mother, who was standing by a stack of men's sweaters, neatly piled on a centrally placed table. She leaned over, looked at the price tags. Briefly, before turning away.

"This is for tourists, Má," Jesús said, and the family started toward the door, Jesús behind them.

As they turned into the corridor, Jesús removed the small, yellow-handled screwdriver he always carried in his right back pocket, gouged it forcefully into the pink plaster wall, like a tiger tearing at an intruder, defending its young. He left a deep elongated groove as he walked along, his signature scratched into the vast hallway, an echo of his wound. Then, before anybody saw him, he made a last stab, caused tiny pieces of pink plaster to fragment and fall to the tiled floor. Then he returned the screw driver to his back pocket.

When they came to the exit door, Jesús's father turned and put his arm around Jesús's shoulders, saying, "Maybe we can come back in a few weeks. I can put up some money for ice cream."

"Yeah, sure, Pa," Jesús answered. But he didn't look his father in the eye.

Construction in Colonia Popular, 1989 (photo by author)

Roofing a house in Colonia Popular, 1989 (photo by author)

— Rigo and his bride, Laura, became my godchildren on the occasion of their wedding in 1992. Prior to his marriage he often came to my house in the colonia, sometimes with other colonia youths, sometimes with Laura, and though not much of a conversationalist, eventually— and over a number of occasions—came out with the following story of his life. It is fictional because I did not capture fully his words but recreated them from my memory.

El Otro Lado: The Other Side

I

1992

This is the true story of a boy named Rigo who lives in a squatter settlement I call "*Colonia Popular*", in Mexicali. It is about how he grew up very fast, retiring from his early career just before turning eighteen, to take a lower paid job as a construction worker. And it is about how his aspirations were formed.

Shortly after they invaded a lot in Colonia Popular, Rigo's father left the family, going away to no one knew where. Rigo's mother was left with nine children, seven of them under twelve. His fifteen and seventeen year old sisters conveniently married within the year. Rigo was the eldest son, and it fell upon him to bring some income into the household. His mother could only earn so much washing and ironing clothes and selling tamales door to door on week-ends. (The children only got whatever was left over after the sales, there was so little money).

One morning she told Rigo, who until then had been going to school: "You'll have to go out and find a job. Any job. It's up to you. You leave in the mornings. You come back when you have earned some money. If you have no money, there'll be no dinner."

And it was thus that Rigo, almost twelve years of age, began selling newspapers in downtown Mexicali. He hitched a ride each morning to make the more than ten mile trip, for the *colonia* where they lived was a poor *colonia*, far from where the better off lived. Located on the city's periphery where even electricity, always the first service available, still had not been installed, the *colonia* turned to mud the few days it rained, even the dirt floors of the houses, as water dripped through the unfinished scrap wood roofs. It was the first permanent home Rigo and his family had ever had, however.

Rigo handed over to his mother most of the money he earned, selling his newspapers in the lanes of cars filled with people carrying documents that let them cross over to the other side, or returning to Mexico. He took only a little to buy himself a taco or two and a soda or a mango or apple from the street vendors whose stalls lined the downtown streets. It was the only time he ate more than beans and tortillas, and an occasional tamale left over from his mother's week-end sales.

He got to know other boys his age, and younger and older, who helped a mother, sister or brother sell inexpensive jewelry, neither gold nor silver except in color, or wooden statues, hair sprays, hand creams and tee-shirts (these latter three from the *Estados Unidos*), flower-decorated hair adornments, key chains and watches, cigarettes and chewing gum, or any other small, low cost item some passer-by might wish to own or consume. A few of the boys sold newspapers, like he did.

Some of the boys hung out in the park after their wares were sold or their work day over or on the way to some errand an older relative had sent them to execute, and they looked through the high chain link fence to Calexico on the other side. Often they saw men crawling up that fence, hanging on to the links while they waited until the uniformed U.S. immigration officer in the tall tower, holding the large semi-automatic rifle under his armpit, looked the other way. They watched the men, and occasionally a woman, scale over the cast iron fence and drop into the parking lot on the other side. The boys watched them walk casually away to meet a new life, a new *camino*, on the other side.

They learned the secret of the two shirts, whereby a crosser would jump the fence in a shirt of one color, then quickly shuck it off and throw it under one of the cars parked in the parking lot, revealing another shirt of a different color. The *migra*, they found, couldn't tell one Mexican from another except by the color of the shirt he wore, so when one of them radioed to another of them to catch the guy with the red shirt who just made an illegal entry, they'd drive past, in their lime green cars or vans, that very guy, now stripped down to a nondescript off-white, or brown, or blue shirt, and walking into the crowded downtown streets into which he disappeared from their view.

The boys also noticed that each morning a number of the same men crossed the fence, then returned, via the fence as well, in the evenings. Rigo was the one who told the others what that was all about, since two of Doña Cuca's brothers from the *colonia*, who sometimes gave him a ride back home, were among them: "They stand out in front of Pronto Market or the California Mercado and trucks and buses come and pick them up and take them out to the fields and there they pick lettuce sometimes, or cabbage, and melons sometimes, and sometimes broccoli."

The boys wondered about crossing themselves. They knew they couldn't get fieldwork until they looked sixteen, but it would be fun to see the other side they thought. To know exactly where the California Mercado was and other stores they heard advertised on the battery run radios in their *colonias*. Blue jeans cost less in the Family Bargain Center than here in Mexicali, they knew. And each of them would have liked to have a new pair of blue jeans.

One of their acquaintances, Marcos, had crossed. Many times, and starting when he was ten-years-old. His widowed mother sold tee-shirts from a booth downtown near where the buses out to the *colonias* stopped. She would send Marcos and his older brother Pablo over the fence each week to buy the shirts in one of the stores in Calexico. They paid ten dollars for three, then resold them at two for ten dollars in Mexicali. At least that what it worked out to be in pesos. Marcos and Rigo would bring the tee-shirts in their plastic bags to one of the holes in the chain link fence and pass them through to their mother, then climb back into Mexicali again.

Rigo wanted very much to know what Calexico looked like, so he tried to convince Marcos, now thirteen, to take him along. "You don't have to pay me nothing. I just want to get to see some place other than here."

Marcos agreed. His brother had been promised work as a car mechanic's helper as soon as he turned fifteen, and that was going to happen in a couple of weeks. As soon as his brother got the job, he'd take Rigo along. If his mother said it was o.k. And she would. "Ma," Marcos told her, speaking nothing but the truth, "if the *migra* catches you it's better to have a buddy along. Because sometimes they yell at you and threaten to hit you or they shake you and its scary."

"All right," Marco's mother agreed. "But just go and get the tee-shirts. No fooling around. Just go and come back, like you always did with Pablo."

And at first that's what they did. They'd scale the fence, walk east four or five blocks part way on first street or all the way on second street, cross Imperial Highway and walk down into the "*hoyo*," the hole, as it was called, and head toward the "Mexicali Tianguis." There they'd load up with at least a dozen tee-shirts, more if Marco's mother had money for more, then walk back across town, past endless rows of stores, back to the chain link fence, where they'd push the packages through to her, then jump back over into Mexico.

Rigo was surprised to find that most people in Calexico were Mexican, and that he could speak Spanish there and everyone understood him, even if some of them talked Spanish in a funny way. Except of course the occasional Anglo shoppers he had no reason to talk to anyway. He decided he wanted to see more than first street and second street and the "*hoyo*." He now knew where the Pronto Market was, because they passed it on the way. But there were other places people had talked about that he hadn't yet seen. Everyone in Mexicali had heard of the Santo Tomás and Las Palmas swap-meets since they were advertised on one of the local radio stations. And one of the women in the *colonia* who had papers used to go over to Las Palmas and bring back second hand furniture and sell it in the *colonia*.

Rigo talked to Marcos and they both talked to Marco's mother. About going to Santo Tomás or Las Palmas to look for tee-shirts. But she said: "No. It's too risky. They're on the other end of town. And who knows if they have tee-shirts?" To end the discussion, she added, partly to herself and partly to them: "And they're probably the same price anyway. Too risky and for nothing."

So they decided to go without her permission. Rigo was the one who asked an elderly Mexican lady they met on the street how to get there. She told them it was far but pointed them the way and replied to his query: "Yes. They sell tee-shirts. Lots of tee-shirts."

Then the two boys walked up Imperial Boulevard and saw the fast food restaurants and the stores and supermarkets, including the California Mercado where men stood in the morning to get jobs as fieldhands, and kept going past the two gas stations, and crossed the east west highway over to the post office and past it to Las Palmas and Santo Tomás. By the time they got there they should have been back at the hole in the chain link fence handing Marco's mother the tee-shirts. But that didn't bother them as much as finding out it would cost them a dollar each to get into the swap meet, also surrounded by a chain link fence, but a lower one, and rather rusty. So they decided to scale that fence too.

When they found tee-shirts at the swap meet were four for ten dollars, they gave each other the knuckle punch handshake all the boys from Mexicali knew, and started picking them out, larges, mediums and smalls.

Marco's mother was distraught when they finally arrived, not noticing at first that there were more shirts than she had sent money for. As soon as his feet touched the soil on her side of the fence, she cuffed Marcos on the ear, while he wailed, over her "Where in the name of God and in the name of the devil have you been?": "Count 'em, Ma. Count 'em. We got them cheaper. We went to Santo Tomás. Me and Rigo."

When her anger subsided with her anxiety, which subsided with the boys' explanations of how easy it all had been, she was pleased. So pleased she gave Rigo a dollar, which he added to his newspaper money to take home to his mother. And from then on he and Marcos went once a week, as always in the afternoons so they wouldn't be picked up as truants from school on the other side, to the Santo Tomás or Las Palmas swap meets to buy tee-shirts.

They got to know Calexico as well as they knew downtown Mexicali. Where every store you could name was and what it sold. They never had money to buy anything in them, but they looked. That the highway they crossed going to the swap meet went east to Yuma and west to San Diego, and that if you continued up Imperial Highway you eventually got to El Centro and further north.

A couple of times they were caught when they jumped the fence into Calexico, and were sent back with harsh words and an occasional kick or back-handed slap. But as soon as they were put through the swinging doors to Mexicali they went back to the fence and scaled it again, cursing the *pinche migra* on the way. Since they were so young they couldn't be detained for long on the U.S. side. Whenever they were caught they always wore a different shirt the next time they crossed, though, so the *migra* couldn't recognize them. And an hour or so each day, after Rigo finished selling his newspapers, and Marcos got a break from the stall, they would hang out with the others in the park.

And they learned more things about the people in the park. They found out that some of the men, and women too, although there weren't many of those, didn't live in Mexicali, but had recently arrived from more southerly states, like Sinaloa and Jalisco and Zacatecas and Michoacán, and hoped to cross to the other side and get up to relatives waiting for them in Brawley or Mecca or Riverside or Santa Ana, or even to Los Angeles or Fresno or Sacramento or Salinas. They discovered there were "*coyotes*" who cruised the park and helped the men and women to get where they wanted to go, for $250 to Los Angeles, more further north. They also learned that the *coyotes* paid "guides" to take the "*pollos*" to places in Calexico where cars or trucks or vans waited to to carry them further north. They paid these guides $50 a crossing, sending no more than one or two people at a time.

Fifty dollars! That was more than a man earned for a week's work at a factory! Rigo began thinking about getting $50 just for jumping a fellow or two and showing them around Calexico.

Soon afterwards Rigo apprenticed himself, when he was almost thirteen, to a *coyote*, and stopped selling newspapers. "You tell where to take the *pollo*, and I'll get him anywhere in Calexico you want," Rigo had announced one morning to one of the men who crossed people to the north.

The man asked him if he knew where the post office was. Yes. Where the FedMart was. Yes. Where the Chevron station was. Yes. Then he said: "O.K. kid. We'll try it. You don't get put in the detention center in El Centro. Too young. So let's see how you'll work out. Tomorrow morning I'll have two *batos* for you to deliver up on the corner of Sixth and Imperial. You'll get half when you go, half when you come back."

So began Rigo's career as a *coyote's* helper. The first day he proudly brought his fifty dollars home to his mother, she knocked him across the room with a fist to his face, then began pounding him with the wooden handle of her broom, across his ribs and back. "I didn't tell you to steal you son of a whore. I told you to work, you *hijo* of your *chingada madre*," she yelled at him, the bills scattering across the earthen floor of their abode.

Rigo didn't tell her where he got the money. "I didn't steal it, Ma," he called out, while rolling on the floor, trying to avoid her blows. "I got it from a man I've been helping downtown." And then he lied, as the beating stopped: "He's going to give me fifty every other week. Helping him to load trucks."

Rigo's mother was immediately repentant, but had forgotten over the long years of abandonment how to show affection or to excuse her temper. She gathered the bills together in silence, folding them and inserting them inside her ample brassiere, then said: "You're no use to me in jail. And I don't want thieves in the family." Then she continued, as if in explanation: "Look at Alejandro's mother. She's always having to pay to get him out of jail. He's always stealing something. All the money he earns, which isn't much, goes to pay to get him out of jail. They even put him in jail now when somebody else steals the stuff."

That night, though, Rigo's mother made an especially nice and seldom seen chicken soup filled with lots of chicken, and she gave Rigo the biggest, plumpest piece, with all the tortillas he wanted, and a liter bottle of soda just for himself alone.

"You should have told me," she growled as she served him. Then she added, she who never gave explanations: "It's going for shoes. The littlest ones need them." And indeed the two littlest ones had no shoes at all, not even the ragged ancient sneakers Rigo and his other siblings wore.

Rigo kept on working for the *coyote*, crossing people for him twice a week, no more than that, so the *migra* would not begin to recognize him. He earned a hundred dollars every seven days for two days of crossing people one or two each day.

II

So his mother would not become worried about how he earned his money, he gave her only fifty dollars every other week. The rest he spent on his friends and two of his younger brothers who had begun coming downtown with him and started selling newspapers. Eventually they found out their brother was a *coyote*'s guide, since they too started hanging out in the park, but they were proud of him and never told their mother.

Some of his money Rigo spent in ways his mother might not have approved of, involving getting to know the pleasures of a cold liter of Tecate beer, bought for the boys by an older man who shined shoes in the park. Some he spent taking his friends and brothers to a certain taco stand where they ate as many *tacos de carne asada* as they wished, filling their bellies with the meat they so seldom saw, while Rigo paid, his face beaming with smiles that had been hidden for much of his childhood. They also started going to see the movies once a week, all in a group, the first time most of them had ever seen one.

Rigo also bought himself a new pair of shoes once when he crossed to Calexico, a pair of black Nikes with white trim costing almost half the price they were sold for in the Mexicali street market. He told his mother that his patrón had given them to him so he could work loading trucks better. He also bought tennis shoes for the two brothers who were working downtown, and he told his mother they were handed on to them by the patrón's two sons, who conveniently had the same sized feet. "Promise me you're not stealing," she said half-angrily when she saw the new shoes. And he swore by the Virgin that he wasn't.

He also bought a fluffy pink dress for one of his sisters' baby girls, and a sleeping bag for his other sister's son. And once in a while he would give a dollar to the Oaxacan family who sat on the street in front of the Hotel del Norte, the husband singing songs while playing a tiny guitar, his wife holding her two small children wrapped in her rebozo, or to the legless man who sat on a wooden plank and begged in front of the Golden State Transport office from where buses crossed to border to take the lucky people with papers as far north as Salinas for less than forty dollars.

When electricity finally came to the *colonia*, Rigo gave his mother the sixty dollars she needed for the down payment to have the wiring extended to their lot. She looked at him suspiciously and thankfully at the same time, when he handed it to her, over and above the usual fifty dollars every two weeks, but she asked no questions. "I got an advance from my *patrón*," Rigo offered in explanation. And he wondered how he could buy a radio-cassette player and bring it to the house without his mother wondering where he got it from. He finally bought one, but left it with one of his married sisters, much to her pleasure, borrowing it from her to play on the corner when he and the *batos* got together.

Rigo still crossed the border with Marcos, or rather Marcos now crossed the border with Rigo. Marco's mother was adamant about not wanting her sons to get involved in crossing people illegally, fearing they might end up in jail. But Marcos crossed with Rigo, to take the *pollos* to their waiting places, staying with them until they entered the vehicles which would transport them further north, then together they went to Santo Tomás and Las Palmas to buy tee-shirts.

Rigo also told the men and women he crossed the secret of the two shirts. Then he'd take them to Marco's mother's stall where they'd buy a tee-shirt to put under whatever shirt or blouse they were wearing, tee-shirts from Calexico, so they could discard their outer garments after scaling the fence and blend like chameleons into the crowded streets of their first stop in the U.S.A.

Rigo worked as a guide for the next four years. He was only caught eleven times in Calexico, four times with men he had crossed over. Each of those four times he was handed over by the *migra* to the Mexican police, who roughed him up, put him in jail, and told him he would have to pay a fine. He always got a message out to whatever *coyote* he was working for, this changing over the years as some moved on and others were locked away for many years on the U.S. side for people smuggling. His current *patrón* would come and take care of his fine, claiming to be an uncle or an elder brother. That meant, in order to pay them back, he would have to cross a number of *pollos* without earning any money, and might go a week or more without being able to take much home. He just told his mother that the *patrón* was unable to pay him until the following week, a common occurrence in all types of small businesses in Mexicali, and considered no more than a temporary nuisance. Eventually he had money again, twice as much a week as his sister's husbands earned working in the foundry near Colonia Popular. As for his occasional day or two absences he excused them by saying he had had to work late and had stayed overnight at the warehouse.

Rigo was glad he always had the company of the *pollos* when he was locked in. The last time he landed in jail, one of the cops made a comment about him: "Hey. Here's what-cha-ma-call-'im again. Thinks we can't recognize him 'cause he keeps changing shirts."

Then, turning to address Rigo: "We know you in any shirt kid. You' ain't playing with the gringos here. You keep coming here we'll have to warm you up," he said, hitting his night stick against his hand.

Some of the *pollos*, most of them, were more scared than Rigo was though. Because their families and friends were further away so they'd have to stay a longer time in the dirty dank jail eating slop and sleeping on the floor than he would, until someone got a collection together to get them out, sometimes taking days to do so, since they weren't crossing the border to go *turistiando* in the first place. And because some macho type on some shift might knock them around a bit, just for fun or to pass the time, knowing they had no recourse since the cops could always claim they took them in under suspicion for smuggling drugs.

Rigo was a few months past seventeen when he was deported from Calexico for the last time. It involved a nasty interaction with two of the *migra*'s officers who caught him, beginning with one saying to the other, in Spanish, so Rigo would hear: "Hey Joe, this guy is getting to look familiar. Should we fingerprint him?"

The one called Joe turned to Rigo: "How old are you, kid?"

His voice steady and eyes defiant, Rigo replied: "Seventeen."

The first officer said, with satisfaction: "Seventeen, huh? Well then, in less than a year you'll be eligible for El Centro. Put you in there a couple of years if you're doing more than picking lettuce. And a couple of months at minimum we catch you hanging around on the street more than twice. And no damned civil rights groupies can protect your damned ass. 'Cause it's the law we'll be applying. No voluntary departures for wetbacks caught three times."

Then, turning to his companion, he directed: "Fingerprint the little snot. We'll keep 'em on file until he's old enough to nail 'im.'"

Rigo knew to give a false name, and the *migra* knew he knew. He was fingerprinted, then pushed, with a kick aimed at his retreating figure by the talkative one of the two, through the revolving doors that spat him back to the Mexican side. Rigo was only glad they had not handed him over to the Mexicali police.

But partially to show he was a bigger man than the cursed *migra* were, he crossed *pollos* two more times, then decided not to keep pushing his luck. He began looking for another job. Everyone knew and he knew, that once a *coyote*'s helper reached eighteen, he was treated as an adult before the law of both countries, and could be imprisoned for many years for smuggling people, even though those people wanted to go, and had friends and relatives waiting for them where they went, and only wanted to find a job to support family members left behind.

The *coyote* he was working for at the time wanted him to continue, for Rigo was a good guide. The *coyote* said he'd even promote him to being a driver, and that Rigo would earn a hundred dollars per person he took up north, and that he'd guarantee he'd spring him if he was turned over to the Mexican police. But he couldn't protect him from the *migra*, Rigo knew. Anyway, Rigo had never learned to drive. Besides, even though his mother had more help now that two of his brothers were working steadily, he didn't want to risk being jailed. He'd be no use to his mother then. She had told him so. On top of it all, more border patrol agents had been put on in the last couple of years, and the job was becoming more dangerous, as his recent run-in had proved to him.

So a few days before his eighteenth birthday, Rigo retired as a *coyote's* helper. He got a construction job, in which he eventually, after six months apprenticeship, earned sixty dollars for six days of dirty, sweaty, but honest labor, forty dollars less than he earned in his previous two day a week career illegally, given reigning law, helping to erase the borderline.

Meanwhile he wondered what Salinas, and Los Angeles, and Santa Ana—where he had an uncle his mother once had told him— looked like and what kind of work he might find there, and if it would pay him more than being a *coyote's* helper. And sometimes, when he went downtown on Sunday afternoons to see a movie, he'd stop by Marco's mother's stall, which Marco's mother's brother who had gotten amnesty for picking lettuce one year when he crossed, was now supplying with tee-shirts. And he and Marcos talked about their experiences in Calexico, and about cities on the other side they'd like to know, and what they'd heard about this place or that.

Store in Colonia Popular, 1991 (photo by author)

Nonfiction Epilogue, 2008

The peso/dollar exchange used in the stories was the "old" peso, which amounted to about 2,200 pesos per dolar.

The Rodina
Over the years Lilia has continued working in the lettuce fields of the Imperial Valley and Salinas, as does her husband. One year her eldest son crossed *sin papeles* (without documents) to work in the Salinas lettuce fields with them, realizing his dream. A year later, at the age of 19, he was killed while working with a friend on the carriage of a semi-trailer truck. Eleven years after the death of her son, Lilia remains extremely depressed about his absence.

La Presidente
For more than a year, in 1995-1996, Socorro worked in San Diego for a woman who paid her 20 dollars a day for housekeeping, about half of the going wage at that time. Later Socorro returned to live permanently in her house in Colonia Popular and found a full-time job which offered her *seguro* (a medical insurance and pension package), sweeping out warehouses for a trucking company. Since she can no longer set her hours, as she could with informal sector work, she has not sought to become president again. Teresa was elected president and served for six months, before retiring in frustration at the factionalism. Socorro and Teresa, along with other women in the colonia, did get the municipal government to put gravel on the roads, after the storm. Nonetheless, residents had to pay the government back for the costs of the section in front of their houses.

Maquiladora Cousins
There were actually three clusters of two cousins each, or six young women from the same extended family, who worked in the maquiladoras, on whom this story is based. One, Laura, married Rigo and intermittently enters maquiladora employment. Her sister remains an unmarried mother and supports herself and her child by working in the assembly plants. Another crossed into the United States with her husband, and now lives in Arizona. Her sister separated from her husband after he began using drugs and became violent with her. She supports her three children by working in a maquiladora plant. A fifth married and hopes to study nursing. She seldom returns to visit Colonia

Popular. The sixth has a happy marriage; she no longer works in the formal sector.

The Cartonero

After working for the Coca Cola company for several years, Martín eventually married. He met his wife at the Coca Cola plant. The couple moved to a nearby colonia, that in other writings I have called La Unión, where they run a small sewing business out of their home.

The Tablaroquero

Jesús later traveled to Los Cabos to work on the Westin Regina and to Guadalajara to work on the Continental Plaza Hotel with his *patrón* (employer) and co-workers from Colonia Popular. He eventually married a woman he met in Mexicali, but after seven years was abandoned by his wife because of his drug use. The Plaza Cachanilla has become a place where working class families, and especially young women and young men, go to walk around to eat a snack and view the shops and one another.

El Otro Lado

Unfortunately for him, Rigo never did get to the other side. This was partially because he had no one to join there. He married at the age of twenty, and within seven years had three children. Given the proliferation of drug use in the *colonia*, and in all the Mexicali *colonias*, Rigo was increasingly caught up in sniffing glue and using other mind-altering substances when he had the money to buy them. He lost his job as a construction worker, because of an altercation with his boss, was employed in the Coca Cola plant for a few months, and then worked loading trucks. For the past eight years has been working as a garbage recycler, collecting cardboard and metals in the dump. The house where he lives with his wife and children is one of the poorest in the *colonia*, and his children roam the streets at night begging passers-by for coins.

About the Author

Tamar Diana Wilson combined poetry, creative non-fiction and academic chapters in her *Subsidizing Capitalism: Brickmakers on the U.S.-Mexico Border* (Albany: SUNY Press, 2005). She has published articles on immigration, the informal sector, and gender issues in *Anthropological Quarterly, Critique of Anthropology, Journal of Borderlands Studies, Human Organization, Latin American Perspectives, Review of Radical Political Economics, Violence Against Women,* and *Urban Anthropology.* Her fiction and poetry have appeared in *Struggle, Anthropology & Humanism, Saturday Night Journal, Thema, Blue Mesa Review* and in two collections of poetry, one edited by Terry Wolverton and one by Candace Catlin Hall. She has lived in Mexico since 1988.

The author, Colonia Popular, 1993 (photo by Palano García)

References Cited

Agar, M. 1990. "Text and Fieldwork: Exploring the Excluded Middle." *Journal of Contemporary Ethnography* 19:1:73-88.
Retrieved from www.cts.cuni.cz/~konopas/liter/Agar-Text%20 and%20Fieldwork.htm, accessed 11/5/05

Cheney, Theodore A. Rees. *Writing Creative Nonfiction: Fiction Techniques for Crafting Great Nonficion.* Berkeley: Ten Speed Books.

Gerard, Philip. 1996. *Creative Nonfiction: Researching and Crafting Stories of Real Life.* Cincinnati, Ohio: Story Press.

Nayaran, Kirin. 1999. "Ethnography and Fiction: Where is the Border? *Anthropology and Humanism* 24:2:134-147.

Root, Jr., Robert and Michael Steinberg. 1999. "Creative Nonfiction: The Fourth Genre." Pp. xxiii-xxxii in *The Fourth Genre: Contemporary Writers of/on Creative Nonfiction,* ed. Robert Root, Jr and Michael Steinberg. Boston: Allyn and Unwin.

Van Maanen, John. 1988. *Tales of the Field: On Writing Ethnography.* Chicago: University of Chicago Press.

Wilson, Tamar Diana. 1992. *Vamos para buscar la vida: A Comparison of Patterns of Outmigration from a Rancho in Jalisco and Inmigration to a Mexicali Squatter Settlement,* Ph.D. diss., Department of Anthropology, UCLA.